DATE DUE			

RICHARD MERAN BARSAM

IN THE DARK

A primer for the movies

THE VIKING PRESS   NEW YORK

First Edition

Copyright © Richard Meran Barsam, 1977
All rights reserved
First published in 1977 by The Viking Press
625 Madison Avenue, New York, N.Y. 10022
Published simultaneously in Canada by
The Macmillan Company of Canada Limited
Printed in U.S.A.

1 2 3 4 5 81 80 79 78 77

Book design by Lucy Martin Bitzer

Library of Congress Cataloging in Publication Data
Barsam, Richard Meran.   In the dark.
Bibliography. p.   Includes index.
Summary: An introduction to movie making,
its history, and criticism.
1. Moving-pictures—Juvenile literature.
[1. Motion pictures]   I. Title.
PN1994.5.B3   791.43   76–58506
ISBN 0–670–39682–6

For WALTER STROHM,
who knows more
about the "picture business" than anyone

acknowledgments

I am grateful to Walter Strohm, Cynthia Norcross Tougas, and David Hyman for their thoughtful reading of my manuscript and for their many helpful comments. And special thanks to Olga Litowinsky, my editor at The Viking Press, for her friendly and encouraging criticism and support. I would also like to thank Mark Berman for his help in typing the manuscript and Mary Corliss of the Film Stills Archive of the Museum of Modern Art for her help in obtaining the photographs in this book. Finally, my thanks to John Crews Rainey and George Nicholson for suggesting I do this book.

R. M. B.

New York City
October 1976

CONTENTS

iNTRoduCTioN

It's fun to go to the movies, to sit there in the dark, to laugh, to cry, to have all sorts of fantasies. From the earliest age we are attracted by the movies because they amuse, excite, and disturb us. Movies also have the power to overwhelm us as no other art form can, except perhaps the total spectacle of a rock music concert or a brilliant ballet or opera production. And the movies can carry us away from the narrow theater seat, and the real world, into the endlessly imaginative world of the filmmaker. We've grown up with the movies, and the movies in turn have grown up with us. For that reason most people take them for granted. At the same time most people have strong feelings about the movies they see— they either hate them or love them—and our favorite movies become a part of us and our lives.

The purpose of this book is to introduce you to the art of the movies and to give you some background for discussion and criticism. For that reason the book is organized into three sections: the first provides an overview of movie history; the second covers the complex business of making a film; and the third is an introduction to film criticism with a detailed look at two important films. The better you understand the movies, the more you will be able to say why you love them or hate them.

THE MOVIES

History

A NEW ART

The movies have been a major form of mass popular entertainment for over three generations. We go to see movies
in theaters, we stay home and watch them on television, we
travel and see them on airplanes and trains, and we study
them in high schools and colleges. Many of us make our own
home movies, and others collect old movies and wouldn't
dream of missing the weekly revivals at the local theater.
Soon movies will be available on cassettes and other recording units—similar to phonograph recordings—so that we

will be able to play and replay our favorite movies anywhere we choose. Movies are being made exclusively for
television, new theaters are being built all over the country,
and audiences are more serious about movies than ever before. The movies are expanding in many ways, but where
they have been is as important as where they are going.

The movies are a part of our history and a part of our
lives, yet the history of the movies is the history of a new
art. Unlike the other arts—painting, music, dance, architecture, sculpture, and literature—the movies were invented
and developed within the last one hundred years. They are
more popular than the other arts, but they share many things
in common. Like painting, they are the personal canvas for
individual, creative directors. Like music, they have tonal
structure and, of course, the movies use music extensively.
Like dance, they move in time and space with freedom,
grace, and control. Like architecture, they enclose human
experiences in structures and give meaning to the life they
contain. Like sculpture, they are almost three-dimensional
with their vivid photography and sound. And like literature,
they tell stories, illuminate characters, enrich myths, and
give meaning to the life around us. The movies borrow from
these other arts to create their own unique, dynamic means
of expression. They are very much a part of the twentieth
century, but the creative spirit behind the movies is as old
as time.

The movies are one of the few things that the ancient
Greeks did not invent, but in a way the philosopher Plato
almost predicted the movies. In his myth of the cave Plato
observes that cave dwellers, when first going out into the
sunlight, are dazzled by the bright light, though they soon
see more than ever before. At the same time, on their first

return to the caves, they have more difficulty discerning its dimly lit objects than their companions who have never looked at anything lit by the rays of the sun. They are simultaneously dazzled by light and dark, and by time and space. In the twentieth century the movie viewer is very much in the same position, for he or she sees things as never before —in new perspectives, in and out of familiar contexts, and, most significant, through the eyes of an artist.

The movies were invented about one hundred years ago, and in that short time they have had an incredibly rich history. Most film historians tend to divide that history into two periods: the silent film era and the sound era. No matter how you divide it, the history of the movies is an exciting story of innovation, development, expansion, and accomplishment.

As an art form the movies combine several basic components: sight, sound, silence, light, dark, movement, and sometimes color. In many ways these components work together to create films of psychological, historical, sociological, and metaphysical interest. In simpler terms, films tell us about people, about the past, about society, and about our relationship with ourselves and the universe around us.

But the primary factor which separates the art of the motion picture from the other arts is its approach to the infinite elements of time and space. The motion picture artist captures time and space within the frame (or borders) of his image (the picture you see on the screen). But at the same time he is able to free his art from these traditional boundaries. With the camera, the editing table, and the optical and sound laboratories to assist him, the artist can jump back and forth in time, can record "real" time in its chronological passing, as well as the "subjective" time that passes in the mind; can move from one space (a room, land-scape, a country) to another; can depict an experience as well as its effect; and can manipulate the rhythms of an event in such a way as to distort, dramatize, or transform it from its original actuality to a new reality on the screen. In short, the motion picture artist is a magician in almost complete control of some of the artistic problems which have confounded other artists for centuries.

In the late seventeenth century Sir Isaac Newton made discoveries which helped to make the nineteenth century Industrial Revolution a reality. As we shall see, the movies were invented in the nineteenth century as a direct result of this worldwide interest in mechanical and technological progress. In the early twentieth century Albert Einstein made scientific discoveries which reinterpreted, for our time, the old problems of time and space. These discoveries of modern physics have made possible much of our technology and most of our scientific progress. Film is a mechanical and technological art, and film artists were able to conquer problems of time and space almost at the same time that scientists were conquering the same problems in the ''real'' and theoretical worlds.

Early filmmakers had to deal with the problems of time and space, but their work was not complicated by ques-tions of sound. The introduction of synchronized sound (keeping sight and sound permanently and perfectly to-gether) brought movie artists right back to the basic prob-lem, for sound images can restrict a filmmaker just as tightly as visual images. Soon sight and sound were fused together in such a way that neither was restricted by the elements of time and space, which otherwise seemed so ty-rannical. Sound helped motion pictures to become more *linear* (in the sense of straightforward storytelling), more *literal* (in the sense that the audience could hear dialogue, sound effects, and music), and more *logical* (since we live in a world of sight *and* sound). The simple, straightforward sound film has been improved by such innovations as color photography, wide-screen projection, multichannel sound recording, and new methods of photography and editing. The movies have changed, and audiences have changed with them; like Plato's cave dwellers, they are no longer fascinated only by flickering images or by the surprise of seeing familiar persons and events on the screen.

Filmmakers must please the audience, for while the movies are an art form, they are, and always have been, a big business. Unlike some of the other arts, the movies are expensive; they cost a fortune to produce, and studios require big profits to enable them to continue production. In the simplest law of economics the supply meets the demand; the audience pays for what it wants, and, for the most part, it gets what it wants. The audience may not always get what it pays for, but that is another problem.

siLENT FiLMS

◑ *The Birth of the Movies: 1815–95* ◑

The movies were not born overnight. Along with many other technological "inventions" of the nineteenth and twentieth centuries, the birth of the movies was foreshadowed by an idea of Leonardo da Vinci's in the sixteenth century. His *camera obscura* was a light-tight box or chamber with a small window in one wall fitted with a lens through which light from external objects entered to form an image of the objects on the opposite wall. It was sometimes used for making drawings, but it was an impractical optical device, and did not really become a workable reality until the invention of photography in the early nineteenth century.

The movies were conceived and born as a direct result of the Industrial Revolution begun in the mid-eighteenth century. During the nineteenth century, three separate mechanical inventions were combined to form the earliest examples of today's familiar motion pictures. These mechanical gadgets were optical illusion toys, still photography, and machines for public entertainment. The toys (called persistence-of-vision toys) employed the optical illusion by which the brain retains images for an instant longer than the eye actually records them. These toys would employ a series of individual pictures (usually on some kind of revolving drum), and the viewer's eye and brain would transform them into a fluid, continuous action. This simple optical illusion is still the basis of the movies, which are made of thousands of individual still photographs printed on continuous rolls of film and projected at a speed which literally "fools" the eye and the brain with the appearance of movement. A quick look at a roll of exposed motion picture film will make this clear.

More important from today's viewpoint was the invention and development of still photography. In 1839, the collaborative experiments of two Frenchmen, Louis Jacques Mandé Daguerre and Joseph Nicéphore Niepce, resulted in the slow but successful method of capturing a photographic image on a metal plate known as a daguerrotype. The Englishman Eadweard Muybridge was the first to adapt these

10

Persistence-of-vision toys: the circular drum of this *Zootrope* (or *Zoetrope*) was fitted with a paper strip of pictures; when the viewer looked at the spinning strip—through the slits in the drum—the alternating moments of darkness and light created the optical illusion of moving pictures.

new still photographs to a very primitive form of motion picture photography. In 1881, he invented the zoopraxiscope, a device which projected pictures on a screen, but remarkable as this machine was, it still did not project motion pictures as we know them. His photographs showed various stages of a single action or event (such as a running horse); these were taken by a series of still cameras placed in a row, not with one motion picture camera running continuously. Motion picture photography was finally invented in 1882 when another Frenchman, Étienne Jules Marey, took the first motion pictures with a single camera. These lasted just a few seconds, but the development of the art was restricted by the limited photographic materials that were then available. Fortunately, new developments occurred soon, for the public was interested in the new gadgets and toys, and inventors realized that a big audience was waiting for motion picture entertainment.

The first real breakthroughs in technology were made in 1888 by two Americans: George Eastman, the inventor of celluloid roll film, and William Kennedy Laurie Dickson, the inventor of the kinetograph, a camera which utilized Eastman's new film for motion picture photography. Dickson was employed by Thomas A. Edison, and although the great inventor eventually patented and produced movie cameras, he did not invent them and was not interested in motion pictures except as a visual accompaniment to the sounds produced by his phonographs. Dickson, who was the most important pioneer in the earliest years of American film development, invented the camera and perfected the projector known as the kinetoscope. Unlike Edison, he saw the potential for the art of the movies, and American film history begins officially with Dickson's first film, *Fred Ott's*

Sneeze (1889), a brief, comic look at Fred Ott, one of Edison's mechanics who made a habit of sneezing on command. Although motion picture photography was invented by Marey in 1882, the preceding years were rich in experimentation and development. With *Fred Ott's Sneeze* in 1889, the public began to respond enthusiastically and film history began to be made.

The American inventors led the way in developing movie film, cameras, and projectors, but two French brothers, Auguste and Louis Lumière, showed the world how to use them. In 1894 they began adapting and improving Dickson's Kinetoscope and Kinetograph (patented by Edison), and their work is important in at least three ways. First, instead of the electric cameras patented by Edison, they invented a portable, hand-cranked camera that could be used anywhere. Second, they slowed their camera so that film would pass through it at 16 frames per second, rather than at 48 frames per second, and this allowed their projector to run more smoothly and quietly. Today 16 mm film, the type used most widely in schools and other nonprofessional showings, contains 40 individual frames (or pictures) per foot of film and runs through the camera or projector at the rate of 24 frames per second or 36 feet per minute (sound) and 16 frames per second or 24 feet per minute (silent). Professional theaters show 35 mm film which contains 16 frames per foot and runs through the camera and projector at the rate of 24 frames per second or 90 feet per minute (sound) and 16 frames per second or 60 feet per minute (silent). Third, the Lumières solved the problem of smooth, clear projection by using the same machine (their Cinématographe) to shoot, print, and project the pictures. The Lumières began making films in 1895. Unlike the Edison

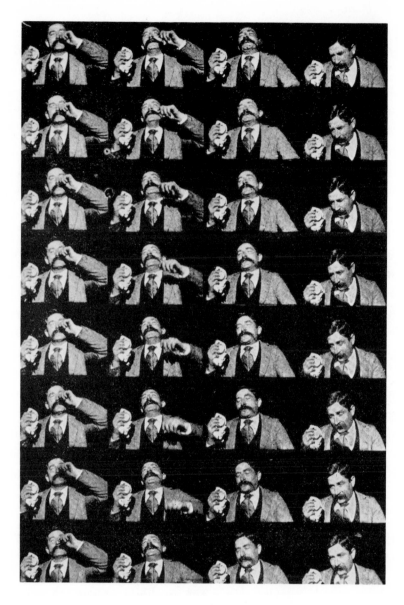

William Kennedy Laurie Dickson's *Fred Ott's
Sneeze* (1889), produced by Thomas A. Edison and here
seen in its entirety, began American film history.

Edison's Kinetoscope machines showed half-minute films, like *Fred Ott's Sneeze*, in elegant parlors such as this one, which opened in New York in April, 1894.

fictional films, the Lumière films were nonfictional films that recorded scenes from the natural world. They did not edit their films and they were not very business-minded about their incredible inventions, but their work and their significance is second only to Dickson's in the first segment of early film history.

◑ The Infancy of the Movies: 1896–1907 ◑

FRANCE AND ENGLAND. By 1895 technical obstacles were overcome, and there was nothing for moviemakers to do but learn how to make better movies. Although the United States led the way in the second decade of the twentieth century, the most important commercial and artistic progress of the first decade was made in France and England.

In France the movement was carried forward by Charles Pathé and his three brothers, and by Leon Gaumont and Ferdinand Zecca; but without question the leader was George Méliès, the movie screen's first great artist. His films used all sorts of magical tricks, including elaborate sets and stop-motion photography (where the camera is stopped while the scene is changed, producing the familiar effect of a picture "coming to life"). Because his staged film productions owe much to the conventions of the theater, they add little to the actual development of the movies, but their humor, showmanship, and inventiveness pleased audiences then and continue to please them now. Anyone who watched the United States moon landing in 1969 will laugh out loud at Méliès's wonderful film *A Trip to the Moon* (1902), for it shows just how young—and how old—the movies really are.

In the Lumières' simple comic film, *L'Arroseur arrosé* (Teasing the Gardener) (1897), the boy steps on the hose, stopping the water; when the gardener stares into the nozzle, the boy steps off the hose, splashing the man.

From George Méliès's fantastic *A Trip to the Moon*
(1902).

In England filmmakers were even more innovative than the French. While Méliès used a camera fixed in one stationary position, they experimented with the moving camera. They also experimented with editing techniques, anticipating, in some instances, the significant developments in photography and editing made in these two areas by the Germans and the Russians in the 1920s.

THE UNITED STATES. The first years of commercial moviemaking in the United States were chaotic ones in which several companies–Edison's and his rivals—were in conflict over patents, production methods, and promotional strategies. It became obvious that the competition was actually hurting, rather than helping, the various companies, and that some sort of organized film industry, with stable policies, was needed. At first the companies agreed to form a monopoly which would control production and distribution, but by 1908 this proved unworkable, and this unsatisfactory situation was complicated by the antitrust legislation passed by the United States Congress in 1890 and 1914. The original plan was for theater owners to buy films directly from producers, but increased public interest forced the theater owners to change programs frequently, and for this reason they wanted to rent films rather than to buy them. Thus the middleman, or distributor, entered the industry; he bought or leased films from producers and, in turn, rented them to theaters. Many theater owners and film producers rebelled against this system and formed their own independent production, distribution, and theater systems. Eventually this organizational chaos led to the establishment of the factory-like Hollywood studios.

This first decade of American film production is not a

memorable one, except for the beginnings of what was to become the studio system and for the films of Edwin S. Porter. Porter studied European films and helped free film technique from the standards set by the stage, but his major influence was in his free handling of editing and combined use of natural and studio settings. Today he is best remembered for *The Great Train Robbery* (1903), the first important Western and the most commercially successful film of its time. By Porter's time the American film was in its infancy, but it had to wait for its first real creative genius before it could approach maturity. With David Wark Griffith that moment arrived.

◑ *The Silent Film: 1908–28* ◐

D. W. GRIFFITH. David Wark Griffith was the single most important force in American film-making between 1900 and 1930, and he is still regarded as one of the greatest—if not the greatest—innovative artists in all film history. His contribution and influence are immeasurable, and with the major exception of sound there was hardly any important aspect of film-making that he did not master. For his own challenge he practically reinvented the old problems of time and space just so he could solve them. He was the first to understand the function of each shot within the framework of the whole film and therefore the first to perceive and to use the "language" of film. He realized that making a film was something like writing a book, because combining shots into scenes, scenes into sequences, and sequences into whole plots was very similar to combining words into sentences, sentences into paragraphs, and paragraphs into finished

Edwin S. Porter's *The Great Train Robbery* (1903) was the first important Western and the most commercially successful film before *The Birth of a Nation* (1915).

compositions. The logic behind this was ''natural,'' and Griffith's feeling for it was natural too. He is the creative father of film, its first intellectual, its first poet, its first success, and unfortunately one of its first failures.

The significance of Griffith's contribution is not that he invented so much but that he improved and combined so many existing techniques into a better method of film-making. He taught his cameramen a wide variety of shots ranging from the extreme close-up (a very large close-up of a subject or object), through the already conventional medium

shot (a human shown from the knees upward), to the extreme long shot (a subject seen in full length or a vast
natural panorama). He exploited the dimensions of the
framed image; in other words, he realized the importance of
the photographic composition of each shot, not only in itself
but in relation to the other shots in the scene or sequence.
He understood the need for editing which would give rhythm
to the film and contribute the necessary mood or feeling.
Griffith developed the "mask" effect in which a shield is
placed over the lens to alter the screen image into a circle,
oval, square, or other shape of light and image within the
frame. He also developed the "iris" effect, named after
the iris of the eye, by which an adjustable aperture on the
camera controls the amount of light reaching the film. With
this iris effect a scene could begin with a small circle of light
within the frame which would then expand to fill the frame,
or a scene could be ended in the reverse manner. Thus the
iris effect is something like the effect made by a spotlight on
a dark stage, for it can pinpoint something in an area of
light and draw the audience's total attention to it. In addition to these changes in the use of the actual camera Griffith
experimented with the pan shot (in which the camera moves
horizontally on its fixed tripod) and the tracking shot (in
which the camera usually moves on a track toward or away
from its subject).

All of this innovation adds up to a few simple, important
points: Griffith recognized the movies as an independent art
form, he freed them from the restraining conventions of the
theater, and he created for himself the almost mythic role
of the film director genius. Between June 1908 and Decem-
ber 1909, at the Biograph Studios in New York City, he
directed two films a week (one was twelve minutes long,

the other was six minutes). His energy was impressive, but so were his films. As we have seen, he revolutionized the technical side of movie production, including lighting and set construction, and he was the first to train actors and actresses for the screen. His company included such silent film stars as Lillian and Dorothy Gish, Blanche Sweet, Mary Pickford, Richard Barthelmess, Lionel Barrymore, Donald Crisp, Robert Harron, and Erich von Stroheim. His early Biograph one-reelers are melodramatic and sentimental, but they are also marked by Griffith's keen observation and understanding of people, their psychology and their inter-relations in society.

Griffith's ideas were less influential than his technical innovations, but the ideas in his films have a tremendous impact on audiences. Although some of his values were tra-ditional ones, others appear naive today. He believed in a world of simple virtue, he saw the family and the home as the cornerstones of society, he believed in gentle, moral peo-ple who lived peaceably and happily together. His faith in these ideas is reassuring, but his view of the world, espe-cially of evil forces, is too simple to be useful today. Griffith was both a dreamer and a realist, and as his one-reelers developed so did the substance of his ideas. His major films —*The Birth of a Nation* and *Intolerance*—are romantic and sentimental, but they also contain flashes of comedy and strong elements of social criticism. His films contain title cards with strong warnings and sentiments; for example, they state that people should respect gentleness and reject violence. This is good advice, of course, and in the relatively quiet years after the turn of the century it must have been comforting advice. But beyond the words the images of the short films tell a more complex story. Griffith needed a larger

23

framework for his ideas, a longer film to contain his moral and social vision of the world. In 1914 Biograph refused to make feature films, and Griffith, like Mack Sennett the year before him, became an independent moviemaker. The year 1914 was the major turning point for Griffith—and for the movies—for it was the year in which he made *The Birth of a Nation.*

The Birth of a Nation (1915) is the most important film ever made. It has earned that distinction for its length and complexity, for its exciting scenes of battle, and for its use of all the technical devices which Griffith and others had developed. At the same time, it has enraged audiences for its picture of America at the time of the Civil War, for its apparent endorsement of the Ku Klux Klan, and for its view of Negroes. *The Birth of a Nation* is the story of a nation split by Civil War, and against the background of the military struggle Griffith tells the story of two families. This human element gives focus to the drama of war and Reconstruction. The struggles and reconciliations of the Northern Stonemans and the Southern Camerons, and the marriage of two of their children, provide the symbolic story of the newly emerging nation.

The problem with *The Birth of a Nation* is not Griffith's vision of a reunited America but his view of Negroes. For Griffith Caucasians are "naturally superior" to Negroes, who are acceptable so long as they know their subservient place in society and keep it. This harsh view is impossible to accept today, and it was impossible for many people to accept in 1915. In fact, the film opened to storms of protest and was banned in some cities. Griffith was not so prejudiced against Negroes themselves as he was against the mixing and marrying between the two races. His villains are not

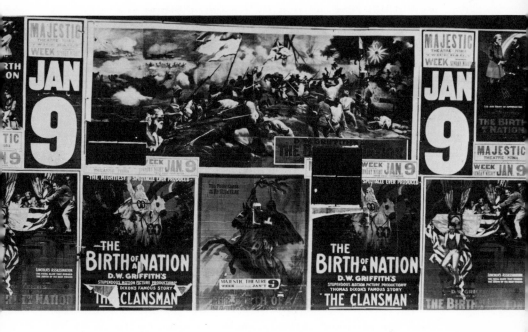

Posters outside the Majestic Theatre (Peoria, Illinois) in January 1916, advertising D. W. Griffith's *The Birth of a Nation* (1915).

pure-blooded Negroes but mulattoes, and they have the same flaws that Griffith saw in the Caucasians that he hated: greed, hypocrisy, and a desire to change social conventions. The film is complex, but one thing is clear: Griffith did not so much oppose the Negroes as the intermarriage of races and the alteration of the traditional white power structure. He opposed slavery, but he also opposed what we have come to call integration.

It is easy to see why *The Birth of a Nation* was both the most controversial and the most successful film of its time. However, the film was popular for other reasons, and its tight construction, suspense, excitement, and tension demonstrated just how successful a motion picture could be in telling a story of many parts. Its crosscutting (the interweaving of shots from at least two episodes or stories during the editing of a film) helped to prove that two separate things could occur on the screen at the same time, just as they do in real life. Griffith extensively used the masking and irising effects, and he used animals as symbols for human emotions and situations. He also provided a musical score (to be played by the theater's orchestra, organist, or pianist) and hand-tinted some sequences with colors to intensify their action and emotion. For those who are familiar only with modern color movies, this delicately tinted film will be surprising, but what is important is that Griffith recognized very early that a perception of color was part of one's perception of reality.

Those of us who love the movies—and who write about them and teach students about them—think that *The Birth of a Nation* is the most important film ever made. We reach this conclusion because of its complex narrative structure, sweeping picture of America, acting, use of settings, extensive outdoor scenes, photography and editing, music, color, and—most of all—its director, D. W. Griffith, without whose vision it would never have been made. The film was one of the most ambitious artistic endeavors in the history of modern art; it took six weeks to rehearse, nine weeks to shoot, and required thousands of men, women, animals, and elaborate indoor sets. It cost $125,000—the most that had ever been spent on a motion picture production. After *The Birth of a Nation* everyone knew that movies were a serious art form, capable of treating serious subjects in a large and impressive manner. But Griffith could not forget that so many people were opposed to his film, and he began to think of himself as the victim of prejudice and intolerance. And so this troubled genius made plans to produce *Intolerance* as the answer to his critics.

Intolerance (1916) did not arouse social protest, and it did not attract large audiences, even though it was the most expensive film yet produced. It cost Griffith the personal fortune he had made from *The Birth of a Nation,* and in some ways it was the highest point of his career, an achievement to which he never returned even though he continued to make films for fifteen years. Despite its lavish sets and costumes, its acting and its ambitious story, it was too complex to appeal to a large audience. The editing of its four stories, rapidly crosscut throughout the film, has had an enormous influence on film-making (and film-editing), but this presentation has baffled many viewers.

Intolerance is about intolerance and injustice, and the emphasis is on Griffith's special view of history and those villains who, in his opinion, have made the world such a violent, vicious place. The four stories are set in Belshazzar's Babylon, in Christ's Judaea, in Renaissance France,

Workers preparing the immense set of Babylon for the Belshazzar's Feast sequence in D. W. Griffith's *Intolerance* (1916).

and in early twentieth-century America. These stories are held together by certain consistent themes, as well as by Griffith's brilliant control of editing. He crosscuts from one story to the next, back and forth, until he brings the film to its four-part climax. Early audiences could not understand this jumping from century to century, from place to place, from one story to another, but modern audiences— raised on films influenced by *Intolerance*—are still overwhelmed by Griffith's handling of this immense and complex adventure. Like *The Birth of a Nation*, *Intolerance* succeeds both as a large and as a small film, excellent in its vast historical pageants and touching in its small human moments. But as with the earlier film, its personal moral vision lacks intellectual depth. But despite its weaknesses *Intolerance* is a colossal, dazzling film which has had a profound influence on the development of the art of the movies.

In two years, between 1914 and 1916, D. W. Griffith created two feature films of such major proportions that his influence is still deeply felt wherever films are made. After 1916 Griffith continued to make films, but he somehow lost his grip on the creative powers that produced his two masterpieces. His later films are less innovative, more sentimental, and hence less appealing to audiences which had quickly become more knowledgeable in their view of the world and in their understanding of movies. World War I made many of Griffith's Victorian ideas of morality seem naive and old-fashioned. Nevertheless, three of his most important films were made during this period, films which pleased audiences then and which continue to please them now: *Broken Blossoms* (1919), *Way Down East* (1920), and *Orphans of the Storm* (1921).

Griffith's final years in Hollywood were marked by bitter

defeat. The businessmen who financed the pictures thought him old-fashioned, and he did little to change their minds. His two attempts to make films with synchronized sound were disastrous, and he was forced—primarily by these financial considerations—to retire in 1930 when he was fifty years old. He lived until 1948, a ghost in the Hollywood world which he had almost single-handedly invented. If his story were not true, it would be the plot for a fabulous movie, the story of a genius of intense morality and technical inventiveness who became the victim of the same intolerance he saw all around him.

◑ The Movies Reach Maturity: 1915–30 ◑

THE STUDIO SYSTEM.   D. W. Griffith was not the only film-maker at work in the early twentieth century, but he was the most important one. As we shall see later, the early comedies were being developed by Mack Sennett and Charlie Chaplin. Griffith, Sennett, and Chaplin were artists who worked for independent studios, mostly on the East Coast, but the major studios were developing at the same time on the West Coast. Films from these studios were less individual in style and theme than those from the independents, but Hollywood wanted regular distribution and thus needed a steady supply of regular films. In the 1930s this was to become the Hollywood "assembly line" type of production, but it had its beginnings around 1915. Audiences wanted certain types of films, and the studios eagerly supplied them: westerns, swashbuckling romances, adventures, domestic melodramas, biblical spectacles, war films, and, of course, comedies.

At the same time that Hollywood was developing these kinds of movies, other familiar aspects of the film industry were also becoming part of the scene. These included the building of ornately decorated movie theaters, the development of the star system, the publication of fan magazines and the first movie reviews, and the first complaints from the popular press about movie morality. The stars' behavior on and off the screen came under public scrutiny. In order to combat the threat of federal censorship and to explain matters to its moralistic critics the Hollywood film industry created its own office of self-control and self-censorship. Starting in 1922 the Motion Picture Producers and Distributors of America (the MPPDA, or Hays Office, as it was named after its head, Will H. Hays) set the standards for screen behavior. It reached its full power in 1934, when its statement of censorship principles was adopted by the industry, and it influenced Hollywood production until the 1960s. By 1925 the following major studios were operating in Hollywood: Paramount, United Artists, Columbia, Warner Brothers, Universal, Fox (later to be known as Twentieth Century-Fox), and Metro-Goldwyn-Mayer.

The major movie directors of the time included Cecil B. De Mille, famous first for his bedroom farces and then for his biblical spectacles, and Erich von Stroheim, an early member of Griffith's acting company. Von Stroheim was a rebellious genius whose film *Greed* (1924) might have been one of the masterpieces of film history if M-G-M had not taken control and cut it to pieces before releasing it. Audiences loved all kinds of films, but they loved the comedies most, and between 1907 and 1930 comedy was king.

31

◑ *When Comedy Was King* ◑

The period in which Griffith flourished and the studio system developed was also the period in which screen comedy was born. Mack Sennett was the first great master of comic films, and he was responsible, partly or fully, for the careers of many of the screen's great early comedians: Charlie Chaplin, Fatty Arbuckle, Marie Dressler, Mabel Normand, Ben Turpin, Billy Bevan, Harold Lloyd, Harry Langdon, and Charlie Chase.

MACK SENNETT. Sennett was the master of slapstick comedy, in which humor is created mainly by scenes showing displays of comic violence or knockabout farce. Sometimes this involves characters who are struck in the face by custard pies or cakes, but Sennett's major contribution was the portrayal of men as if they were machines. His famous characters, the Keystone Cops, summed up Sennett's passion for speedy, zany action, filled with hitting, kicking, crashing, and flying pies, bricks, and other objects. His favorite targets were the respectable figures of society—preachers, professors, society ladies, and the police—and he delighted in making fools of all of them. His great gift was the ability to see through everyone and everything, to reduce it all to one great laugh.

CHARLIE CHAPLIN. Chaplin learned much from Sennett, but he was destined to take screen comedy in a new and different direction. While Sennett turned people into objects, Chaplin turned objects into living creatures. Where Sennett saw the world as a silly place, Chaplin saw injustice, greed, and inhumanity. Almost from the beginning he saw life

32

through the eyes of the famous tramp figure that he was to immortalize, but in order to express his view of things he had to leave Sennett's Keystone Studios and work on his own as an independent producer and director.

Between 1915 and 1920 Chaplin made many comedies for several different studios, and in that time he began to perfect the style of his later masterpieces. His greatest contribution was that he took comedy seriously; his films had control, unity, and a serious point of view. They were filled with improbable situations and audiences loved them, but they made their points about the world and left the audience thinking while it was laughing.

Chaplin's silent films were well-developed expressions of his comic vision and artistry. For one thing, the films were longer, varying from two to six reels (a two-reel film ran for thirty-two minutes); for another, he had begun to perfect the tramp figure. By 1922, when he started making full-length features for United Artists, he was in full command of his style, and it was in this period that he made one of his most popular films, *The Gold Rush* (1925). Here the little tramp's warmth and humanity is all the more out of place in the world of snow and ice. The film's comic moments (Charlie cooking and eating his shoe, for example) are balanced by its pathetic moments (Charlie jilted by the girl of his dreams on New Year's Eve). He wins in the end, but only by accident; what is important about *The Gold Rush* is its story of human survival.

With the introduction of sound Chaplin took his little tramp to even greater fame. His later films (discussed later in this section) were wonderfully funny, but they also did what comedy does best by pointing out the lack of justice, tolerance, and humanity in the world.

In a moment of pathos in *The Gold Rush* (1925), Charlie Chaplin encounters the women who have forgotten his dinner invitation on New Year's Eve.

BUSTER KEATON. Although Chaplin and Keaton developed
at the same time, no two comedians could be more different
in comic style and effect. Chaplin was slow, intimate, and
often quite sentimental. Keaton was fast, zany, and famous
for his deadpan face. He was an excellent gymnast, an accomplished mimic, and despite his small size and delicate
stature he was a comic hero who succeeded. Chaplin's tramp
invariably lost everything but the audience's hearts, while
Keaton's heroes invariably won their battles. A Keaton
character was no less lovable than a Chaplin character, but
he was more practical, more determined, and more resourceful. In his best film, *The General* (1928), Keaton shows these
characteristics at their best. It is a film of great charm, portraying a little character of great strength, and it stands
along with *The Gold Rush* as one of the best comic films of
our time.

During the 1920s, in addition to Chaplin and Keaton, the
Keystone Cops, and the various stars of Sennett's short
films, Harold Lloyd, Harry Langdon, and Laurel and Hardy
enjoyed great success with their films. Lloyd is best known
for his horn-rimmed glasses, and for his thrilling ability to
get himself out of situations of great physical danger. He
was neither as subtle nor as intellectual as either Chaplin
or Keaton, but he had a great sense of the sight gag, and
with films like *Safety Last* (1923) and *The Freshman*
(1925) he achieved great popularity with the public. Harry
Langdon made a comic career out of being a stupid, incom-
petent clown. His simple, innocent nature got him into situations he could not understand or control, but he always
managed to win. Langdon's character added something that
the other comedians lacked. They always won by their skill
or their determination, but he always won by luck. It is no

Buster Keaton (as Johnny Gray) in *The General* (1928), prepares to load the cannon being pulled behind the locomotive of his beloved train.

surprise that he was popular, for most of us would like to believe that the good, simple person always wins even if by good luck. Stan Laurel and Oliver Hardy were the perfect comic team. Their short films are well structured, tightly controlled, and highly predictable exercises in which a silly, single problem gets carried away to zany, hysterical conclusions. They love to break things apart, to tear things down, and to get into all kinds of physical trouble. Laurel is sad-faced and pathetic, and Hardy is jovial and lovable. Together they are two childish brats who cry when they don't get their ways, and who love pulling each other's hair. Each is clumsy and graceful, and their classic approach to comedy has earned them a special place in the hearts of movie fans.

◐ Early Nonfiction Films ◐

The film history of the 1920s is generally remembered for the work of Griffith and the comic masters, but the nonfiction film was also being developed at this time. These films provide a cinematic document of an actual happening; at first they were called factual films and later they were called documentary films, but today films which are factual rather than fictional are generally known as nonfiction films. As we have seen, the first films ever made—those of Dickson and the Lumière brothers—were nonfiction films, and hundreds of films have been devoted to nonfiction records of various historical events.

Flaherty's *Nanook of the North* (1922) was not the first American nonfiction film, but it was the first full-length film

Robert Flaherty's *Nanook of the North* (1922), a
nonfiction film account of Eskimo life, includes this
tender moment in which Nanook warms his son's hands
after teaching him some tricks with a bow and arrow.

of its kind to achieve wide popular success. It is a simple, silent film of great personal charm, and one that remains popular with audiences today. *Nanook* tells the story of an Eskimo family and its daily fight for existence in the frozen Arctic. Flaherty is impressed by Nanook's versatility, and he makes a true hero out of him, but the strength of the film is not this fascination with Nanook but Flaherty's objective presentation of another culture. His second film, *Moana* (1926), was an attempt to make the same kind of film about South Sea island life, but it was not as successful as the first. Flaherty's later nonfiction films, *Man of Aran* (1934), *The Land* (1941), and *Louisiana Story* (1948)—the latter is discussed in full in the last section of this book—are perfect examples of his ability to record a way of life while revealing his own attitudes toward it.

From this brief review we can see that American movie-making in the 1920s was characterized by geniuses and giants, by technical innovators who pushed the silent film as far as it could go, by comic masters who made us laugh as they made us think about our world, by budding actors and actresses, fast-talking producers and distributors, and by writers and directors who made great successes by knowing just what the public wanted to see. It was the age of Griffith, Chaplin, Flaherty, and others—a golden age of adventure films, comic films, epic films, and nonfiction films. There was no sound yet, no color (except for Griffith's experiments with tinting parts of *The Birth of a Nation*), no animated cartoons, and no wide-screen projection. But there was just about everything else, from big studios to temperamental artists, and in the United States as well as around the world the movies were becoming a part of everyday life.

◐ *European Movies: 1900–30* ◐

Looking at movie history in two simple parts—the silent era
and the sound era—we can see that the United States led
the way, pioneered the technique, and dominated the movies
from the beginning of the silent era until the introduction
of synchronized sound, which was also an American invention. But, as we have seen, there was important activity and
invention in other countries too, especially in France in the
late 1890s. However, the influence of American film-making
was felt around the world as European filmmakers studied
Griffith's developments while creating their own techniques.
Generally speaking, European film-making has always been
more experimental and more forward-looking than its American counterpart. While American moviemakers have almost
always tried to please the widest possible audience, European filmmakers have tended toward broadening the art
form and giving it more intellectual and artistic substance.
And there is one obvious reason for this. From the beginning Americans adopted the movies as an important form
of public entertainment; until the invention of television,
at which point the movie industry almost collapsed overnight, going to the movies was an integral part of American
life. Europeans have a much older and more traditional
culture, with easy access to other arts and art forms, and
they thought of the movies as an art rather than a business.
Since World War II the situation has changed, and movies
have become extremely popular in Europe as well as around
the world, but in the years before 1940 European filmmakers
made movies without worrying about the box office.

FRANCE. French film-making in the 1920s provides a good

example of this distinction between European and American film-making. During this period such directors as Abel Gance, René Clair, Jean Renoir, Jean Cocteau, the Spaniard Luis Buñuel, and Jean Vigo were experimenting in France with the new art, and painters such as Man Ray, Marcel Duchamp, Fernand Léger, and the Spaniard Salvador Dali were also expanding the ways in which film could be used. The period is notable for such films as Gance's *Napoleon* (1927), Clair's *The Italian Straw Hat* (1927), and the notorious surrealist film by Dali and Buñuel, *Un Chien Andalou* (*An Andalusian Dog,* 1928). Perhaps the most important film of the decade was made by a Dane then working in France. Carl Theodor Dreyer's *The Passion of Joan of Arc* (1928) is famous for its haunting close-ups and formally composed images. If we could put only two silent films in a museum, the choices most likely would be *The Birth of a Nation* and *The Passion of Joan of Arc*, for together they take the silent film about as far as it can go. Each is a masterpiece in its own way, and neither needs sound to tell its story, enhance its moods, or enrich its emotions. And few actresses know as much about emotion as Griffith's star Lillian Gish or the French actress who played Joan, Renée Falconetti.

SCANDINAVIA.   In the Scandinavian countries there was less experimentation than in France but more emphasis on creating a mood in films which showed man's relationship to nature, his metaphysical existence. The great directors were Carl Theodor Dreyer (*Leaves From Satan's Book,* 1920), Victor Sjöström (*The Phantom Chariot,* 1920), and Mauritz Stiller (*The Treasure of Arne,* 1919). Stiller's film *The Story of Gösta Berling* (1924) is important not only for its epic

41

Joan of Arc (Renée Falconetti) being hounded by
the inquisitors in Carl Theodor Dreyer's silent film *The
Passion of Joan of Arc* (1928).

retelling of a famous Swedish novel but for one of its stars: Greta Garbo. Although Garbo had already appeared in one feature (*Peter the Tramp*, 1922), it is now lost, and *Gösta Berling* is considered the first important film starring this legendary actress.

GERMANY. While French films of the silent period emphasized visual experimentation, and Swedish films were characterized by natural moods, the German film was noted for its dark, emotional power, rich, suggestive settings, and bold, symbolic stories. Like the Americans, the Germans concentrated on films produced in well-equipped studios rather than on films shot on location. Thus sets, lighting, decor, and costumes were very important elements in their films. During this period, prior to the rise to power of Hitler and the Nazi party, creativity flourished at UFA, the great German film studio. Among the important directors there were Ernst Lubitsch, F. W. Murnau, Fritz Lang, and G. W. Pabst; among the important films were Robert Wiene's *The Cabinet of Dr. Caligari* (1919), a mystical horror film of great visual beauty; F. W. Murnau's *Nosferatu* (1922), the first screen version of the Dracula story; Fritz Lang's *Metropolis* (1926), a fantastic vision of future life, said to be Hitler's favorite film; and Murnau's *The Last Laugh* (1924). The German public also admired a less artistic sort of film devoted to romantic stories involving much skiing and mountain climbing; these "mountain films" were especially popular during the late 1920s and gave Leni Riefenstahl, the great German director, who was then a dancer and actress, her first opportunity to make movies. The Germans were also experimenting with the abstract film (one in which form, movement, and color are more sig-

The Vampire (Max Schreck) in F. W. Murnau's
silent German film *Nosferatu* (1922), the first screen
version of the Dracula story.

nificant than story content), as well as the nonfiction film, an area in which Walter Ruttmann's *Berlin: The Symphony of a Great City* (1927) is an influential classic.

THE SOVIET UNION.   Early Soviet film history is distinguished by two things. First, Soviet films were intended for propaganda and instruction rather than for entertainment. Second, the Soviets developed theories of editing which are still dominant today. Editing is the process of assembling a film from available shots and sound track. The Russians applied the term *montage* to this process, but their important early work was with silent, not sound, film. Russian experiments in editing were carried out by Lev Kuleshov, Sergei Eisenstein, Vsevolod Pudovkin, Alexander Dovzhenko, and Dziga Vertov. For the Russians montage was the fundamental creative process in making a film. They built on the editing discoveries of D. W. Griffith but also added their own important innovations, the most significant of which perhaps was their discovery that editing can combine shots of apparently unrelated material so as to generate new, meaningful relationships within the minds of the audience.

Eisenstein was the master of what the Russians call dynamic montage, a fast-paced, dazzling combination of images. The most impressive and most famous example of this technique is the ''Odessa steps'' sequence from his *Potemkin* (1925). The film depicts the workers' revolt of 1905 by focusing on the rebellion of the crew of the battleship *Potemkin* in the bay of Odessa. The workers of Odessa joyfully support their comrades' actions; some of them sail out to the ship, while others remain on shore, watching the action from the steps which lead down to the water. Sud-

A medium close-up from the electrifying "Odessa steps" montage in Sergei Eisenstein's *Potemkin* (1925).

denly the czar's troops march down the steps and systematically kill every person in their path. The terror and drama of this scene is portrayed with a series of different kinds of shots, from a variety of locations, and paced with a horrifying rhythm. The scene depicts the mass murder, but its political emphasis is as important as its cinematic energy, for it portrays the crowd as innocent victims and the soldiers as bloodthirsty barbarians. Eisenstein manipulates the emotional rhythms of the film and thus the emotional reactions of the audience. The film time for the sequence is longer than the action would have taken in actual time; the difference of course is in the editing dynamics by which Eisenstein adds rhythm, power, and impact to the scene.

Pudovkin and Dovzhenko were the other masters of early Russian film-making, and while each learned from Eisenstein, each was different in his contributions to film technique. Pudovkin placed his cinematic emphasis on individuals, not on the masses, and made important advances in the use and placement of the camera. His films include *Mother* (1926), *The End of St. Petersburg* (1927), and *Storm Over Asia* (1928). Dovzhenko, a Ukrainian, was the poet of Russian cinema, relying on the images and the montage, not on the story, to convey the meaning of his films. His most important films are *Zvenigora* (1928), *Arsenal* (1929), and *Earth* (1930). Among the other early innovators of Russian film-making were Dziga Vertov, famous for his *Man with the Movie Camera* (1929); Abram Room, whose domestic comedy *Bed and Sofa* (1927) was a departure from the political propaganda of other films; and the two nonfiction filmmakers Victor Turin (*Turksib*, 1929) and Esther Shub, notable as one of the first women filmmakers in the world and famous for her experiments with montage which combined old newsreel footage.

sound films

◐ *The Importance of Sound* ◐

By the late 1920s the silent film had developed fully into a sophisticated and rich art form that did not lose any of its value because it lacked sound. But two factors helped to change the course of movie history. First, the inventors and technicians were experimenting with sound and reached by the late 1920s a satisfactory way to add sound to sight images. Second, the public wanted sound, and because the film industry was always eager to give the public what it wanted, it was just a short time before fully synchronized sound films became the rage, and silent films were all but forgotten. Movies were revolutionized in the switch to sound, for the whole process of film-making had almost to be reinvented to accommodate the new invention.

The silent and the sound film are different from each other in many ways other than the obvious one. The technical aspects of making a sound film involve a whole new range of equipment and methods. The addition of sound— voices, music, sound effects—creates a whole new area of communication that does not exist in the silent film. And the sound film requires a redefinition of the idea of the movies, for in addition to using new techniques it requires the filmmaker to integrate sight with sound images. For the first time, with the coming of sound, the world on the movie screen not only looked but also sounded like the real world.

◦ *The Idea of Sound* ◦

Sound movies were "invented" in the late 1920s, but the idea of adding sound to motion pictures was almost as old as the idea of the movies themselves. In his early work at the Edison Labs William K. L. Dickson experimented with synchronizing sound to picture. Edison had invented the phonograph but was not interested in motion pictures except as an accompaniment for the music that his phonograph produced. He did not see the possibilities for joining sight and sound images to create a wholly new form of entertainment. In this Edison was not looking far enough into the future; he correctly predicted that the phonograph would be popular, but he remained stubborn about the potential for movies, in general, and sound movies, in particular.

The early Dickson experiments could not overcome the two major obstacles to satisfactory sound film production: synchronization and amplification. The process of synchronization is the process of keeping the photographic and sound images permanently and perfectly together. Amplification is the process by which sounds are made loud enough to be heard by an entire auditorium of people. The problem of synchronization was solved by the invention of the oscilloscope, an electronic device that converts sound waves into light beams. These light beams become the sound track, a narrow band of one side of the strip of celluloid film which carries the recorded sounds accompanying the images. The problem of amplification was solved by Lee De Forest's invention of the audion tube, a device which, in combination with loudspeakers, made possible the wide-scale broadcasting of sound later in theaters and over radio waves.

49

Between 1906, the year of De Forest's invention, and 1927, the year of *The Jazz Singer*, there were a variety of attempts to produce a satisfactory film which synchronized sight and sound. Perhaps the two most important were those with the trade names of Movietone (sound on film) and Vitaphone (sound on disc). The Movietone process was purchased by William Fox in 1927; the Fox Studios began producing a series of films which featured short conversations with famous people as well as the first newsreel series, the Fox-Movietone News. In 1925 the Warner Brothers Studio purchased the Western Electric Vitaphone system; by 1926 they were producing short films featuring musical performances. But it was the year 1927 that marked the first real breakthrough in sound film. *The Jazz Singer* (1927) was neither the first "talkie" nor the first film which synchronized sight and sound, but it was the first to integrate sound into the narrative of the film. Prior to *The Jazz Singer* sound had been used as an accompaniment to the picture, not as an integral part of it. Now there was actual dialogue to replace the title cards (the printed text which previously told us what was happening or what people were saying); now there was actual music coming out of Al Jolson's mouth rather than a "canned" sound track played over the theater speaker system or a score played by the theater orchestra. Although *The Jazz Singer* is essentially a silent film with passages of dialogue and song, its effect on audiences and on the film industry was incredible.

Within two years after *The Jazz Singer* all studios converted their production facilities to enable them to make sound films. But the conversion was not an easy process for several reasons. First, it was very expensive. Studios had to invest in new equipment—sound cameras, microphones, amplifiers, processing laboratories—and had to build new sound stages (large studio buildings where indoor shooting takes place). These sound stages are soundproofed to keep out noise from the outside and to insure the best possible recording inside. Second, movie theaters had to be converted to enable them to project sound films. New projectors, amplifiers, and speakers had to be installed. Third, existing production methods had to be adapted to sound filming. Sound cameras were very large; this restricted camera movement and made it difficult, at first, to take life-like shots. Microphones were very clumsy so actors and actresses had to stand close to hidden microphones and speak directly into them. This whole cumbersome process is delightfully spoofed in the musical *Singin' in the Rain* (1952). Fourth, the coming of sound created new jobs, but it also put people out of work. Many directors could not make the change; D. W. Griffith, for example, was out of work by 1931. Many actors and actresses who were accustomed to silent films could not make the change either. They had never learned to speak or sing properly because it was never required of them. To help solve the problem Hollywood hired new writers, who could write acceptable dialogue, and new directors who would see that their actors and actresses spoke as convincingly as they moved. Some stars made the transition from silent to sound films with ease; others retired and were replaced by actors and actresses from the stage, where speaking was as important as moving. Billy Wilder's *Sunset Boulevard* (1950), starring Gloria Swanson, offers a harsh view of the effects of sound on a silent film actress.

Billy Wilder's *Sunset Boulevard* (1950) tells the
story of a famous silent-screen star who did not survive
the transition to sound production. Here Norma Desmond
(Gloria Swanson) and her lover (William Holden) watch
one of her old films and plan her comeback in sound.

◎ *Early Sound Films* ◎

The directors of early sound films had many problems, but the biggest one was in deciding how much and when to use sound. Some scenes are improved with sound (either talk, music, natural effects, or a combination of all), and some are better left silent. Sometimes it is better to hear something but not to see it on the screen, and at other times it is necessary to see and hear the person or thing at the same time. To overcome the fact that the new sound cameras were not as mobile as silent cameras, directors would shoot some scenes first and then dub the sound in later (dubbing in this case means dialogue that is recorded after photography and then added to the sound track of the film). Directors all over the world experimented with sound, and although the United States dominated sound with its well-organized studio system, the major advances in sound film production were made in Europe.

◎ *European Sound Films* ◎

The Germans and the French led in the production of sound films in Europe. The Russians were far behind, and Eisenstein did not complete a full-length sound film until 1938. The Germans were ready early, for their silent production relied on studio filming, and these large studios could be easily adapted to the production of sound movies. Josef von Sternberg, an American, was imported from Hollywood to make *The Blue Angel* (1929), his second sound film, in Germany; it makes brilliant use of sound, and for the first time audiences were able to hear Marlene Dietrich talk and sing. Other important German sound films include Fritz

The first German sound film was Josef von Sternberg's *The Blue Angel* (1929), starring Marlene Dietrich.

Lang's *M* (1931) and G. W. Pabst's *Westfront 1918* (1930). Almost all important German film directors had fled Germany by the time Hitler came to power in 1933, and German film-making in the Nazi period followed the repulsive lines of party propaganda and is cinematically uninteresting, with a few exceptions. The most important of these films is Leni Riefenstahl's *Triumph of the Will* (1935). It is a propaganda masterpiece, but its flattering portrait of Hitler is much less interesting than its montage, and the film is one of the most important turning points in the editing tradition begun by Eisenstein and the Russians. Her *Olympia* (1938) is not a propaganda film but a mammoth record of the 1936 Olympic Games and one of the most cinematically exciting documents in film history.

With their interest in film experimentation, the French eagerly plunged into sound film production. Like the Germans, they understood that silence can be as effective as sound, and that nonsynchronized sound had its own values. The French directors mastered the principles of sound more quickly than the Germans, certainly more quickly than the Russians, and went on to make outstanding films. Among these are René Clair's *Under the Roofs of Paris* (1930), *Le Million* (1931), and *A Nous La Liberté* (1931); Jean Renoir's *La Chienne* (1931), *Boudu Saved from Drowning* (1932), and the later masterpieces, *Grand Illusion* (1937) and *The Rules of the Game* (1939); Jean Vigo's *Zero for Conduct* (1933) and Jean Cocteau's *The Blood of a Poet* (1931). Each of these directors continued to make films during the sound period, leaving his distinctive mark on the history of film.

The Americans may have produced the largest number of films in the largest studios, but the French produced

some of the best films of all time before the end of World
War II. Films such as Renoir's *The Rules of the Game*
(1939) and Marcel Carné's *The Children of Paradise* (1944)
are not just great sound films but film masterpieces.

◐ *American Sound Films* ◐

From its beginnings Hollywood was an entertainment factory; it existed to mass produce a sufficient number of films
to entertain the millions of people who went to the movies
each week. Between 1930 and 1950 the Hollywood studio
system produced over five hundred feature-length films each
year (a feature film runs for at least one hour) and dozens
of cartoons, shorts, and newsreels. These movie factories
were organized like all factories; each department had its
specific task, and each contributed its part to the whole—
the finished film. As we shall see in more detail in the next
part of this book, movie-making involves a great deal of
teamwork between dozens and sometimes hundreds and
thousands of people. Behind the finished product that we
see on the screen are countless technicians and specialists
who help to keep the assembly line moving. Today that
studio system has almost vanished, but in its prime—between 1930 and 1955—there was nothing quite as fabulous
as a Hollywood studio in full production.

Hollywood produced movies in the same way and for the
same reason that Detroit manufactured cars; the assembly-
line method was used to make large profits. Like cars made
on the assembly line, most Hollywood movies were new,
sleek, fashionable, and well within the limitations of the
audience's budget. Unlike custom-made cars, they were

sometimes undistinguished, monotonous, and boring. But the studios existed to create a product of reliable quality, at a predictable speed, and on a predictable budget. Considering the restrictions of this system, it is no small miracle that Hollywood was frequently able to produce films of quality. Most of the films that came out of Hollywood during this period were just fine for the millions in the audience; some of these films reached a higher standard of quality because they were made by a highly gifted director, or written by an imaginative writer, or acted by genuine artists. These American masterpieces can stand comparison favorably with the films of any country, and many of them are the films that today we call classics.

The entertainment factory in Hollywood excelled in producing films of certain types: westerns, biographies of famous people, gangster films, comedies of all kinds, historical romances; in addition, the coming of sound made it possible to produce musical films. During the 1930s and 1940s the major studios in Hollywood were Metro-Goldwyn-Mayer (M-G-M), Paramount, Warner Brothers, Twentieth Century-Fox, RKO, Walt Disney, Columbia, and Universal; in addition to these there were several smaller studios, including Goldwyn, Monogram, and Republic, and several studios devoted to producing animated films (cartoons). But the two giants were M-G-M and Paramount, and each produced a very different type of film. M-G-M was famous for its stars, for its management (the dictatorial Louis B. Mayer and the gifted producer Irving Thalberg), and for its magnificent productions. Its "stable" of stars included Judy Garland, Joan Crawford, Greta Garbo, Jean Harlow, Mickey Rooney, Clark Gable, and Spencer Tracy. On the other hand, Paramount was famous for its directors, for giving its producers freedom from centralized policy-making, and for productions which dared to challenge the standards which M-G-M often took for granted. Each of the other studios excelled in one or more kinds of films; for example, the most famous gangster pictures came from Warner Brothers; the most exciting adventure films were made at Twentieth Century-Fox; and the scariest horror films carried the Universal Studios name.

If you thought that such specialization meant that the film was more important than the people who made it, you would be right to a certain degree. The major studios each had a stable of directors, writers, designers, and actors on constant call, and each of them was expected to work on any kind of picture. An assignment was an assignment, and a person under contract to a major studio had to accept what was offered. We can find many cases where some stars would work only in the sorts of movies with which they were identified, but, for the most part, the stable provided a constant supply of flexible professional people. The legendary stars continued to make films which carried on their legends, and there are a variety of complex psychological and sociological reasons for their existence, but, in a commercial sense, they existed to give the public what it wanted. For example, the public wanted Judy Garland musicals, and it got Judy Garland musicals. When M-G-M cast her in another kind of picture—for example, Vincente Minnelli's *The Clock* (1945), in which she did not sing—they took an artistic and therefore a financial gamble. In this instance the gamble turned out to be lucky, for *The Clock* is a simple, pleasant film which shows Garland's acting ability under the masterful direction of Minnelli. In later years Garland played major dramatic roles in such films as *A Star Is Born*

(1954), *Judgment at Nuremberg* (1960), and *A Child Is Waiting* (1962).

Since Hollywood has always been famous for its "stars," we tend to think of movies in terms of them, but we should not neglect the many other creative talents behind each film. Most of all the public neglects the director, the man or woman who is often the most creative force in the making of a film. It is the director whose talents give a film its distinctive qualities. With many Hollywood films, the name of the director is often unimportant or forgotten, but with others, the name of the director is all-important and remembered as long as the film is shown. These directors are the ones who put their personal stamp on films by avoiding the obvious, by insisting on quality, and by assuming complete artistic control of the production. Some of the great Hollywood directors of the 1930s and 1940s were Ernst Lubitsch, Josef von Sternberg, Rouben Mamoulian, Michael Curtiz, Howard Hawks, John Ford, Frank Capra, Mervyn LeRoy, George Cukor, Walt Disney, Charlie Chaplin, Orson Welles, and Alfred Hitchcock.

ERNST LUBITSCH.   Lubitsch became famous for making intelligent, comic films about sex. They did not break the standards set by the 1934 production code (from the Hays Office), and measured by today's standards, they would not bother anyone. In fact, Lubitsch was famous for avoiding specific subjects and situations that might attract the censors; he was sophisticated and clever, but most of all he was funny about a subject that many people in the 1930s would neither accept nor understand as a natural human activity to be mentioned on the screen. Lubitsch's films include *The Love Parade* (1929), his first sound film; *Trouble in Paradise*

(1932); *Ninotchka* (1939), starring Greta Garbo; and *To Be or Not To Be* (1942).

JOSEF VON STERNBERG.   Von Sternberg was also famous for making movies about love and sex, but unlike Lubitsch's witty, cynical films, the films of von Sternberg depicted passionate situations in exotic, foreign settings. He was born in Brooklyn, but he began his career in Berlin, where he discovered Marlene Dietrich and made *The Blue Angel* (1929), the first German sound film. Dietrich and von Sternberg made seven films together, and she symbolized all that his movies were about. She was glamorous, mysterious, attractive to men; his films were ornate, symbolic, and romantic; and his style fit her style perfectly. Their films include *Morocco* (1930), *Dishonored* (1931), *Shanghai Express* (1932), *Blonde Venus* (1932), *The Scarlet Empress* (1934), and *The Devil Is a Woman* (1935).

ROUBEN MAMOULIAN.   Trained on the Broadway stage, Mamoulian was brought to Hollywood to make *Applause* (1929), one of the first sound films. Later he made *Becky Sharp* (1935), the first three-color feature-length film in Technicolor. In Hollywood he adapted quickly and was particularly innovative in his approach to sound and the use of the camera. When he returned to Broadway, he revolutionized the American musical comedy with his landmark production of *Oklahoma* in 1943. His other films include *Love Me Tonight* (1932); *Song of Songs* (1933), with Marlene Dietrich; *Queen Christina* (1933), with Greta Garbo; *High, Wide and Handsome* (1937); *Golden Boy* (1939); and *Blood and Sand* (1941). He began the filming of the spectacular *Cleopatra* (1962), with Elizabeth Taylor, but was replaced by Joseph L. Mankiewicz.

Greta Garbo in *Queen Christina* (1933), directed by
Rouben Mamoulian.

MICHAEL CURTIZ. Like Lubitsch, Curtiz was imported to
Hollywood from Germany. Like other studio directors—
William Dieterle, Lewis Milestone, Victor Fleming—Curtiz
was completely professional and adaptable, and his long list
of films includes some diverse classics: *The Charge of the
Light Brigade* (1936); *Santa Fe Trail* (1940); *Casablanca*
(1942), with Humphrey Bogart, and one of the most popular
films of all time; *Yankee Doodle Dandy* (1942), with James
Cagney; and the Joan Crawford classic, *Mildred Pierce*
(1945).

HOWARD HAWKS. Hawks is known as the director of outdoor
action films and indoor comedies, but unlike Lubitsch, von
Sternberg, and Mamoulian, he did not emphasize sex or
romance. Instead, his films concern the conflicts between
people of integrity and include some of the best films of the
early studio years: *Twentieth Century* (1934); the wonderful *Bringing Up Baby* (1938), with Katharine Hepburn and
Cary Grant; *His Girl Friday* (1940); *Sergeant York* (1941),
an all-time classic with Gary Cooper; *To Have and Have
Not* (1944) and *The Big Sleep* (1946), two Humphrey Bogart
films. After World War II, he made westerns, including
The Big Sky (1952), *Rio Bravo* (1958), and *El Dorado*
(1966); comedies, including *I Was a Male War Bride*
(1949) and *Gentlemen Prefer Blondes* (1953), with Marilyn
Monroe; and adventure films, including *Hatari* (1962), with
John Wayne.

JOHN FORD. Ford was probably the most adaptable studio
director in the history of Hollywood. Like Hawks, he was
interested in stories of the old West; with his unique style,
he brought to the screen the basic conflicts of good and evil

Paul Henreid, Ingrid Bergman, and Humphrey
Bogart in Michael Curtiz's *Casablanca* (1942).

Howard Hawks directed Katharine Hepburn and
Cary Grant in *Bringing Up Baby* (1938).

which marked the movement across the Great Plains, through the deserts, to the sierras. Since 1920 Ford has directed about 175 films, including such famous westerns as *Stagecoach* (1939), *My Darling Clementine* (1946), *Fort Apache* (1948), *She Wore a Yellow Ribbon* (1949), and *The Man Who Shot Liberty Valance* (1962). But Ford's career was not limited to making westerns, and some of Hollywood's most distinguished films are his, including *The Informer* (1935), *The Grapes of Wrath* (1940)—which is discussed in detail in the last section of this book—*Tobacco Road* (1941), *How Green Was My Valley* (1941), *The Quiet Man* (1952), *The Long Gray Line* (1954), and *The Last Hurrah* (1958). Ford's influence and reputation are second to none; like D. W. Griffith, he made films which expressed his unique vision of the world. Unlike Griffith, he did not indulge his personal feelings and grudges but rather stressed goodness, kindness, and compassion.

FRANK CAPRA.   Both Ford and Capra were interested in American morality, but Capra's films were different because he believed that everybody could be nice if given the chance to be nice. The sentimental and folksy attitude of his films was enormously appealing to audiences in the Depression and during World War II. A Capra film is sincere, honest, and usually very entertaining, but unlike a John Ford film, it lacks a timeless moral focus. His most memorable early films include *It Happened One Night* (1934), *Mr. Deeds Goes to Town* (1936), *Lost Horizon* (1937), *Mr. Smith Goes to Washington* (1939), and *Meet John Doe* (1941). During the war he produced the superb nonfiction film series *Why We Fight* (1943–45), a government-sponsored series of propaganda films designed to inform Americans and their allies

Claude Rains and James Stewart in Frank Capra's
Mr. Smith Goes to Washington (1939), a sentimental,
idealistic view of democracy in action.

of the reasons behind the war. After the war Capra was not as active, but his films include *State of the Union* (1948), *A Hole in the Head* (1959), and *A Pocketful of Miracles* (1961).

MERVYN LEROY. LeRoy was another studio director who could be counted upon to create many kinds of films with consistent style and quality. His long filmography includes *Little Caesar* (1930)—with Edward G. Robinson, the first important gangster film—*I Was A Fugitive From a Chain Gang* (1932), *Tugboat Annie* (1933), *Anthony Adverse* (1936), *Madame Curie* (1943), *Thirty Seconds over Tokyo* (1944), *Quo Vadis* (1951), and *Million Dollar Mermaid* (1953). In addition to his role as a director LeRoy has also served as producer for many important films. His films are as distinctive as those of other professional studio directors —such as William Wellman, Leo McCarey, Preston Sturges, and W. S. Van Dyke—but his career lasted from the beginning of sound through the 1960s, and that in itself is worthy of mention. The Hollywood studio system was a cruel one to directors, and very few of them lasted as long, or made as many good films, as Mervyn LeRoy.

GEORGE CUKOR. Cukor, like Mamoulian, went to Hollywood from the Broadway stage and is also known as one of the best directors of women in films. Cukor has directed Jean Harlow (*Dinner at Eight*, 1933); Greta Garbo (*Camille*, 1936); Katharine Hepburn (*Bill of Divorcement*, 1932, *The Philadelphia Story*, 1940, *Adam's Rib*, 1949, and *Pat and Mike*, 1952); Judy Holliday (*Born Yesterday*, 1950); Judy Garland (*A Star Is Born*, 1954); Marilyn Monroe (*Let's Make Love*, 1961); Audrey Hepburn (*My Fair Lady*, 1964); Maggie Smith (*Travels with My Aunt*, 1972); and Elizabeth

Mervyn LeRoy's *Little Caesar* (1930), the first gangster film in sound, featured Edward G. Robinson as Rico.

Taylor, Ava Gardner, Jane Fonda, and Cicely Tyson in
Bluebird (1976). Cukor is known mostly for his comedies,
but he has done adventures, musicals, romances, and adaptations of great novels (such as *David Copperfield*, 1934).
He is unique among studio directors in that he has not
directed a typical western, although his *Heller in Pink
Tights* (1959), with Sophia Loren, is a comic approach to
the period western. Cukor directed many scenes in *Gone
with the Wind* (1938) but was removed from the film and
replaced by Victor Fleming, another studio director, who
also made *The Wizard of Oz* (1939). Like Mervyn LeRoy,
Cukor has had a long, distinguished career of making memorable Hollywood films.

WALT DISNEY. Unlike the other filmmakers mentioned in this
section, Disney was not just a director. He was a dreamer
in the largest sense, and it is difficult to draw a clear line
between his ideas and the actual work of the many skilled
animators who created the brilliant cartoons that carry his
name. The Walt Disney studio was as complex and as
organized as M-G-M, and although it was never as large, it
was responsible for some of the most charming, most memorable, and most colorful films ever made. The early sound
films included Disney's *Steamboat Willie* (1928), not only
the first Mickey Mouse cartoon to be shown publicly but also
a remarkable example for later makers of sound films to
follow. His use of color was equally important, for it brought
the world of dreams and fantasies to life. Classic cartoon
features from the Disney studios include *Snow White and
the Seven Dwarfs* (1937), *Pinocchio* (1939), *Fantasia*
(1940), *Dumbo* (1941), *Bambi* (1943), *Cinderella* (1950),
Alice in Wonderland (1951), and *The Lady and the Tramp*

(1956). The Disney studio has also made many feature films with live actors, as well as documentaries and short cartoons. The Disney feature-length animated films are classics in every sense of the word; their stories, their colorful presentation, and, most of all, their brilliant animation reserve for them a special place in film history. The live-action features are not particularly interesting, for they are an obvious attempt to make entertainment for the whole family, but they have been enormously successful at the box office. The world of Walt Disney is a world which almost every child in the world enters sooner or later, and it is a world to which adults return with fond memories.

CHARLIE CHAPLIN. Chaplin was not the traditional Hollywood studio director, for he remained an independent director and producer all his life. His output of sound films has been small, in contrast to his reputation, but his influence on comedy has been second to none, and his tramp figure is perhaps the most widely recognized character in all movie history. With his first two sound films (*City Lights*, 1931, and *Modern Times*, 1936) he made a reluctant switch to the new technique after a very active period of making silent films, and even his later films rely more on his pantomime than they do on words and music. Chaplin's feature-length sound films include *The Great Dictator* (1940), *Monsieur Verdoux* (1947), *Limelight* (1952), *A King in New York* (1957), and *A Countess from Hong Kong* (1966).

ORSON WELLES. Welles came to the attention of the moviegoing public with *Citizen Kane* (1941), which is, in my opinion, the greatest film ever produced in a Hollywood studio.

No director has captured the audience's attention more completely than Orson Welles, and no director has had such an impressive beginning, yet Welles's method of working was not compatible with the studio system. He was forced out of Hollywood soon after he made *Citizen Kane*, and he has made films independently all over the world since that time, but they have never reached the stunning brilliance of that film.

Citizen Kane is important for many reasons. Its flamboyant story covers the life of Charles Foster Kane, a publisher whose life bears a distinctly obvious similarity to the life of William Randolph Hearst. But its style is more important than its subject. The narrative structure of the film is far more complex than the traditional American film, but Joseph L. Mankiewicz's script develops the story with perfect clarity. In 1916 audiences were not ready for the interweaving and crosscutting of four stories in Griffith's *Intolerance*, but in 1941 they were more than ready for Welles's telling of the Kane story. The photography breaks the rules in almost every scene, and, as a result, brings to film-making some of the most important innovations ever made. For example, some scenes are shot from below floor level, and others are shot in extreme deep focus (a focus in which all objects from close foreground to distant background are seen in sharp definition). Welles also made extensive use of the moving camera and of theatrical lighting. And there are important breakthroughs in other areas of the film, from lighting and settings to music, narration, and acting style. *Citizen Kane* is sharply critical of the American way of life and especially of those (like Kane) who are in a position to manipulate people. But ultimately it is not the story of America but the story of one man's individuality, greed,

Orson Welles (standing left) as Charles Foster Kane in *Citizen Kane* (1941). The scene was shot in extreme deep focus so that all objects from close foreground to distant background are seen in sharp definition.

Gregg Toland's photography for *Citizen Kane* included scenes shot from below floor-level, such as this one showing Joseph Cotten (Jed Leland), Orson Welles (Kane), and Everett Sloane (Mr. Bernstein).

loneliness, and despair. *Citizen Kane* is as fresh and exciting today as it was when it was made; like *The Birth of a Nation*, it is timeless.

Citizen Kane is Welles's masterpiece, but he has also directed *The Magnificent Ambersons* (1942), *The Lady from Shanghai* (1947), *Macbeth* (1948), *Othello* (1951), *Touch of Evil* (1958), *The Trial* (1962), *Chimes at Midnight* (1966), *The Immortal Story* (1968), and *F Is for Fake* (1975). In addition, he has acted in countless films. As actor,

director, writer, and designer Welles has little competition.
If he had made nothing but *Citizen Kane*, he would stand
with D. W. Griffith as one of the great innovative geniuses
in movie history.

ALFRED HITCHCOCK. Although Hitchcock is British, he has
spent the major part of his career in Hollywood, where he
has been the absolute master of the crime thriller film which
combines suspense and comedy. A Hitchcock film is immedi-
ately recognizable by its fast plot, strange and often amusing interruptions, and ironic twists of fate. He understands
film completely, as indicated by his brilliant way with photography, sound, and editing. A complete listing of his films
would be extensive, but some memorable titles are *The
Thirty-Nine Steps* (1935) and *The Lady Vanishes* (1938),
both made in Britain; then, in Hollywood, *Rebecca* (1940),
Spellbound (1945), *Notorious* (1946), *The Paradine Case*
(1947), *Strangers on a Train* (1951), *Dial M for Murder*
(1954), *Rear Window* (1954), *To Catch a Thief* (1955),
Vertigo (1958), *North by Northwest* (1959), *Psycho* (1960),
and *The Birds* (1963). Hitchcock also produced and occa-
sionally directed a long-running television series of myster-
ies. His influence on crime thrillers has been as vast as
Chaplin's influence on comedy films, and like all great
directors, Hitchcock is in complete control of his own special
world, a world in which the eccentric and the ordinary blend
in a way that is both horrifying and amusing.

◎ *Nonfiction Films* ◎

This discussion of sound movies between 1928 and 1945
would not be complete without mention of the continuing

development of the nonfiction film. Although nonfiction films were not made within the conventional studio system (except during World War II when the studios were producing films for the war effort), they developed alongside the feature-length fictional film and, with the coming of sound, became very important especially in the late 1930s and during World War II.

Between World Wars I and II the world underwent vast changes, one of the most important of which was a new awareness of international relations and, as a result, a new awareness of different cultures. As we have seen, Robert Flaherty was among the first filmmakers to respond to this with his films *Nanook of the North* (1922) and *Moana* (1926). But it was not until the early 1930s, with the world-wide Depression, that nations took a serious look at themselves, at their neighbors, and at their interrelationships. A major factor in these relationships was trade, as it always had been, but the interdependency of countries in a time of economic chaos was more apparent than it had ever been before. Living in a nation with many colonies, the British were among the first to recognize this; they were also among the first to produce nonfiction films which dealt with immediate social problems.

The British nonfiction film movement, sponsored by the government, was led by John Grierson. Between 1930 and 1940 a small group of filmmakers produced a large number of outstanding social "documentaries" on every subject from housing to pollution to city planning. Among these filmmakers was Alberto Cavalcanti, Humphrey Jennings, Harry Watt, Basil Wright, and Paul Rotha. They experimented extensively with sound, especially with live recording and narration, and their films are impressive examples of the power of the nonfiction film form. Among the important titles are *Night Mail* (1936), *North Sea* (1938), *Fires Were Started* (1943), and *Target for Tonight* (1941).

The American nonfiction film movement started later than the British, it was not government sponsored (except in part for a brief time), and it was not as successful in reaching the public. While American nonfiction filmmakers tackled similar problems, especially those dealing with agriculture, they did not reach as wide an audience as the British. For one thing, Americans are a little suspicious of "idea" films; for another, there were just too many people to reach. A small country like England can arrange the distribution of government-sponsored films so that almost every community would have a chance to see them; but in a large country like America, with independent production and distribution, it was not so easy to reach all the people. The leader of the American movement was Pare Lorentz; his films *The River* (1937) and *The Plow That Broke the Plains* (1936) are unique American statements and are still shown widely today. Other important filmmakers in the American movement include Willard Van Dyke (*The City*, 1939), and the Dutch-born filmmaker Joris Ivens (*Power and the Land*, 1940). In the late 1930s two important and influential experiments in "screen journalism" were introduced: *The March of Time* and *This Is America*. Both series were shown in public theaters and did a massive job of informing and preparing the American public about the issues prior to the outbreak of World War II.

During the war the nonfiction film came into its own as the governments of involved countries realized the power of film to educate and to persuade. In England and in Hollywood all film production was geared to the war effort, and

David and Albert Maysles used the direct nonfiction
film approach in the making of *Grey Gardens*.

although the studios continued to make feature fiction films, they also recruited many important directors, writers, and stars to make nonfiction films to inform the public about the important issues surrounding war and peace. Among these films are John Ford's *The Battle of Midway* (1942), Frank Capra's series *Why We Fight* (1943–45), William Wyler's *Memphis Belle* (1944), and John Huston's *The Battle of San Pietro* (1945).

◐ *The Movies After World War II* ◐

Just as the history of the movies can be divided into two basic periods—silent and sound—the sound period can again be divided into two periods: 1927–45 and 1945–75. The dividing line is, of course, the end of World War II. The war changed world boundaries, world thought, and world destiny. It also changed the ways in which people thought about each other, and in a smaller way, the movies in which they looked at each other. In the United States and around the world the movies would never be the same as they had been. Techniques of production changed, audiences changed, but, most of all, the nature and purpose of the whole movie idea changed. After World War II the movies matured.

UNITED STATES.   The postwar years in Hollywood were chaotic. During the war the major Hollywood studios continued to make the sort of entertainment films that they had always made, except that they added references to the war to build morale. People needed the movies to divert them, if only for a few hours, from the horrible reality of the war. After the war the audience expected movies to return to the old task of entertainment, but instead, they were attracted, amused, and informed by a new medium: television. In its early days television had even fewer good programs than it does today, but it had two major advantages over the movies: the audience could stay at home to watch, and, outside of the initial investment in a television set, it was free.

Making movies and making television programs are two different things. As we shall see, the movies are made through a fairly simple process involving mechanical equipment, while television is made through a fairly complex process involving electronics. But the differences between the two processes are more apparent on the screen than in the studio. A television image does not have the visual beauty, the spatial sense, the fusion of image and sound that makes movies an art form. With very few exceptions, involving gifted artists working with television in an experimental way, television as we know it is still not an art form. For most Americans the television set is a source of continuous entertainment, but television broadcasting is still in its infancy compared to the art of the movies. Equally important, television is even more under the control of businessmen; movies are made to make money, but television programs are made to sell products. Almost everything in television is subordinated to the commercial message.

As television captured more and more of the movie audience the major studios began to suffer and, eventually, to die. In a determined effort to attract people back to the theaters Hollywood experimented with new production methods. Eventually films became more serious, with more concern for real issues, but Hollywood's first reaction to the threat of television was not to offer stories that were more mature but to offer gimmicks that the small television screen could not offer. By the mid-1950s a number of experiments had been tried: 3-D (three-dimensional projection for which the audience had to wear uncomfortable plastic glasses), Cinerama (an extra-wide screen projection system), CinemaScope (another wide-screen process), Smell-O-Vision (a projection system which actually sprayed different odors into the theater). These wide-screen processes were visually exciting and gave rise to a series of spectacular films: *This Is Cinerama* (1952), *The Greatest Show on Earth* (1952), *The Robe* (1953), *The Ten Commandments* (1956), and *Ben Hur* (1959), to name only a few of the most successful early ones.

While Hollywood was converting to the wide screen it was also developing multichannel and stereophonic sound systems. Another change was the almost total shift to color photography; Hollywood needed color to compete with black-and-white television, and this kept audiences coming back to the theaters until the late 1960s when color television was perfected. As the studio system continued to break down and eventually to die out independent producers began to make their mark on film history. An independent production is a film that is made without the financial backing of an established film studio. The producer obtains funds from other sources—usually from banks—and then contracts to use studio facilities often in return for distribution rights.

While general audiences were lost to television, a new movie audience began to develop. People who believed that film could be serious still wanted to see films, and this gave birth to the so-called underground film movement in America; also, it encouraged foreign directors to show their films here. In short, the situation involved changes throughout the world of film: changes in production, distribution, exhibition, promotion, and make-up of the audience. Millions stayed at home to watch television, but there was still an audience for the new independent films, for the underground films, and for the films from foreign countries.

In Hollywood many of the great directors of the 1930s and 1940s—John Ford, Howard Hawks, George Cukor, Walt Disney, and Alfred Hitchcock, among others—continued to make films that were solid professional entertainment. But the newer Hollywood directors proved to be equally professional and competent in turning out mass entertainment. They include John Huston (*The Maltese Falcon*, 1941, *The Treasure of the Sierra Madre*, 1948, *The Asphalt Jungle*, 1950, *The African Queen*, 1951, and *Beat the Devil*, 1954); Elia Kazan (*A Tree Grows in Brooklyn*, 1945, *Gentlemen's Agreement*, 1947, *Pinky*, 1949, *Viva Zapata*, 1952, and *On the Waterfront*, 1954); Stanley Kramer (*The Defiant Ones*, 1958, *Inherit the Wind*, 1960, and *Judgment at Nuremberg*, 1961); Vincente Minnelli (*Meet Me in St. Louis*, 1944, *An American in Paris*, 1951, *The Band Wagon*, 1953, and *Gigi*, 1958); Otto Preminger (*Laura*, 1944, *The Moon Is Blue*, 1953, *Bonjour Tristesse*, 1958, and *Advise and Consent*, 1962); Preston Sturges (*Sullivan's Travels*, 1941, *The Miracle of Morgan's Creek*, 1943, *Hail the Conquering Hero*, 1944, and *The Beautiful Blonde from Bashful Bend*, 1949); George Stevens (*I Remember Mama*, 1947, *A Place in the Sun*, 1951, *Shane*, 1953, *Giant*, 1956, *The Diary of Anne Frank*, 1959, and *The Greatest Story Ever Told*, 1965); Billy Wilder (*Double Indemnity*, 1944, *The Lost Weekend*, 1945, *Sunset Boulevard*, 1950, *Stalag 17*, 1953, *Love in the Afternoon*, 1957, *Witness for the Prosecution*, 1958, *Some Like It Hot*, 1959, and *The Apartment*, 1960); William Wy-

Tony Curtis, Jack Lemmon, and Marilyn Monroe in
Billy Wilder's *Some Like It Hot* (1959).

ler (*The Best Years of Our Lives*, 1946, *The Heiress*, 1949, *Roman Holiday*, 1953, *The Desperate Hours*, 1955, *Friendly Persuasion*, 1956, and *Ben Hur*, 1959); Joseph L. Mankiewicz (*A Letter to Three Wives*, 1949, *All About Eve*, 1950, *Julius Caesar*, 1953, *The Barefoot Contessa*, 1954, *Guys and Dolls*, 1955, *The Quiet American*, 1957, *Suddenly Last Summer*, 1960, and *Cleopatra*, 1962); and Fred Zinnemann (*The Men*, 1950, *High Noon*, 1952, *The Member of the Wedding*, 1953, *From Here to Eternity*, 1953, *Oklahoma*, 1955, *A Hatful of Rain*, 1957, *The Nun's Story*, 1958, and *A Man for All Seasons*, 1967).

Most of these new directors made films that are characterized by one thing: straight, realistic scripts presented with straight, realistic style. Some of these films deal with subjects that had never before been treated on the screen: alcoholism, unfaithful wives and husbands, handicapped soldiers, sexual deviations, drug addiction, postwar injustice, and violence.

Critics are always commenting on the subject of the movies' violence, to name only one aspect of the society around them, and we can trace the increased depiction of violence on the screen to the years following World War II and the Korean War. The Vietnam War has added another historical perspective, and after these bloody years audiences have become accustomed to seeing physical violence and brutal death. Western and gangster films, especially, reflect this fact of American society. Producers know that violent films get people out of the house and away from the television set, where they are not always able to see the same sorts of ugliness as are permissible on the movie screen. The public appears to want violence, perhaps because it is used to it, perhaps because the bloody scenes in

Warren Beatty and Faye Dunaway in Arthur
Penn's *Bonnie and Clyde* (1967), a film that provoked
much discussion of violence in the movies.

The French tradition prospered until the early 1960s when the New Wave, a movement of young film critics and directors, swept tradition out to sea. The New Wave was led by Jean-Luc Godard, François Truffaut, Roger Vadim, Louis Malle, Alain Resnais, and Claude Chabrol; their films combined a variety of cinematic styles into one film, and they used disjointed time sequences and spontaneous, even improvised, acting with a freedom that made them visually surprising, intellectually compelling, and consistently entertaining. Their most important films include Godard's *Breathless* (1960), Truffaut's *Four Hundred Blows* (1959), Vadim's *Les Liaisons Dangereuses* (1959), Malle's *Zazie dans le Métro* (1960), Resnais's *Hiroshima Mon Amour* (1959) and *Last Year at Marienbad* (1961); and Chabrol's *Les Biches* (1968). These founders of the new movement in French cinema have gone on to make different types of films, each in his own style, but they continue to reflect the stylistic currents of the New Wave.

Postwar Swedish film is best known for the work of Ingmar Bergman. He began his prolific career in the theater, and his most popular films—often made with the same company of actors—express his personal philosophy, psychology, and mythology. Bergman's brilliant stories, and his unique way of telling them through film, have made him one of the major forces in world cinema along with Fellini, Buñuel, Truffaut, and others. His most important films to date include *The Seventh Seal* (1956), *Wild Strawberries* (1958), *The Magician* (1959), *The Virgin Spring* (1960), *Through a Glass Darkly* (1962), *The Silence* (1962), *Persona* (1965), *The Passion of Anna* (1969), *Cries and Whispers* (1973), and *Scenes from a Marriage* (1974).

Besides the new movies made in Italy, France, and Swe-

French New Wave: François Truffaut's *Four Hundred Blows* (1959) features Jean-Pierre Léaud as Antoine Doinel, an adolescent caught in an adult world.

den, new developments in the film art were being made after the war in England, Czechoslovakia, Japan, and India. The British reputation for solid, realistic films was carried on by such directors as David Lean and Carol Reed, and British comedy flourished with the many films of Alec Guinness (*Kind Hearts and Coronets*, 1949; *The Lavender Hill Mob*, 1951; *The Captain's Paradise*, 1953, and others). Although the British never experienced any film movement as important as Italian Neo-Realism or the French New Wave, their films changed in the late 1950s and early 1960s with the films of Jack Clayton (*Room at the Top*, 1959) and Tony Richardson (*Look Back in Anger*, 1959, *The Entertainer*, 1960, *A Taste of Honey*, 1961, *The Loneliness of the Long-Distance Runner*, 1963, and *Tom Jones*, 1963); and later with the films of Lindsay Anderson (*This Sporting Life*, 1963, and *If*, 1968).

The work of Luis Buñuel is an excellent example of post-war European film production. Born in Spain, Buñuel made surrealist and experimental films in the French avant-garde movement of the 1920s and 1930s. Between 1945 and 1960 he made films in Mexico mostly, and during the 1960s and 1970s he returned to Europe to make films in several countries. He is truly an "international" filmmaker, creating his grimly comic vision of life in whatever country offers the funds and facilities for production. Buñuel is particularly critical of religious hypocrisy and middle-class morality, and while his films take place mainly in Spain or France, they have a universal appeal and popularity. He has made over thirty films, including *Nazarin* (1959), *Viridiana* (1961), *The Exterminating Angel* (1962), *Diary of a Chambermaid* (1964), *Belle du Jour* (1966), *The Milky Way* (1969), *The Discreet Charm of the Bourgeoisie* (1972), and *The Phantom of Liberty* (1974).

In Eastern Europe the Czechs, Poles, Yugoslavs, and Hungarians made comic films which expressed awareness and criticism of the social changes going on around them, and they also excelled in the neglected art of animation. In Japan the films of Akira Kurosawa opened up a world that had long been overlooked by the West. Kurosawa's films were either Samurai epics (such as *Rashomon*, 1950, and *Yojimbo*, 1961) or stories of modern Japan (such as *Drunken Angel*, 1948, and *Ikiru*, 1952). The flourishing Indian film industry was as much a mystery to the West as was the Japanese film industry, but the moving films of Satyajit Ray opened a world of great wonder; he is best known for his "Apu" trilogy (*Pather Panchali*, 1954, *Aparajito*, 1956, and *The World of Apu*, 1959).

◑ *The Movies Today* ◑

The movies are here to stay, not only as mass entertainment, but also as a serious art form. A new generation thinks of the movies, along with rock music, as its own means of expression. Students take film courses in high school and college, and the new, inexpensive film-making equipment has encouraged young and old alike to become amateur film-makers. Movies are being studied and written about seriously, and as already mentioned, movies will soon be available on cassettes and other recording units—similar to phonograph recordings—so that we will be able to play and replay them anywhere. Functional new theaters are being built in places like shopping centers to replace the ornate movie palaces of yesterday. Independent production is booming, and while the quantity of films is lower than it has been in previous years, the quality is often superb. The first-rate films are given first-run showings in quality houses; the others are given saturation screenings in large groups of theaters and then often sold to television, where many of them appear within a year after commercial release in theaters. Now even prestigious films like *The Godfather* (parts I and II, 1972 and 1974) are sold for television screening. Also important are the movies made to cater to special-interest groups and to minorities that, in the past, had to be content with films produced for a mass audience. For example, there are films made by and for the black audience, films made exclusively for rock music fans, and a wide range of films showing various sexual experiences.

Many contemporary films tend to be international productions, rather than the product of a single studio in a single country. The creative personnel, the casts, and, most of all, the financing come from many sources. This development has freed the movies from many restrictions, but it has also opened new frontiers and gained larger audiences. Today's movies strive for honesty and realism in subject and style. Scripts are bold, taking us further into areas of psychology, sociology, history, and metaphysics than films have ever probed before. The leading characters in these films likewise experience a range of activities and express a range of emotions that are almost totally unlike those depicted in earlier films.

Techniques of production have changed also. Directors have learned much from the Italian Neo-Realists and from the French New Wave about the use of real people (instead of actors), actual locations (instead of studio settings), and disjointed time (instead of chronological storytelling). The camera has become much more mobile, especially with the increased use of the zoom lens, and sound recording has become an exciting art all its own. The gimmicky innovations of the 1950s have disappeared; in their place are

93

Robert Altman's *Nashville* (1976), a cinematic vision of American society and its values, was the result of unprecedented collaboration between the director and his actors and actresses, many of whom wrote their own dialogue and songs.

beautifully photographed, beautifully recorded, wide-screen films in color, films which rely on quality, not on gimmicks, for their appeal.

The way to the future of the movies is characterized by these developments, but most of all by the new di-

rectors and their films. It is still too early to chart
the currents of contemporary movie history, but its
movement is marked by such American films as Arthur
Penn's *Bonnie and Clyde* (1967), Stanley Kubrick's *2001:
A Space Odyssey* (1968) and *Barry Lyndon* (1976), Sam
Peckinpah's *The Wild Bunch* (1969) and *Straw Dogs* (1971),
George Roy Hill's *Butch Cassidy and the Sundance Kid*
(1969), Bob Rafelson's *Five Easy Pieces* (1970), Peter Bogdanovich's *The Last Picture Show* (1971), Martin Scor-
cese's *Mean Streets* (1973), *Alice Doesn't Live Here
Anymore* (1975), and *Taxi Driver* (1976), Francis Ford
Coppola's *The Godfather* (parts I and II, 1972 and 1974),
and Robert Altman's *Nashville* (1975). The changing development of the movies is further influenced on a worldwide
scale by directors such as Ingmar Bergman, Federico Fellini, Luis Buñuel, Michelangelo Antonioni, François Truffaut, Lindsay Anderson, and John Schlesinger. And the
restrictive lines which have separated the nonfiction and
fiction film are being challenged and creatively broken by
such innovative nonfiction film makers as Alfred and David
Maysles (*Salesman*, 1969, *Gimme Shelter*, 1970, and *Grey
Gardens*, 1976); Frederick Wiseman (*High School*, 1968,
Hospital, 1969, *Basic Training*, 1971, *Juvenile Court*, 1973,
and *Welfare*, 1975); Marcel Ophuls (*The Sorrow and the
Pity*, 1971) and Peter Davis (*Hearts and Minds*, 1974).

The movies have come a long way since the days of Dickson, Lumière, Flaherty, and Griffith, but there is no end in
sight to their growth and development. The movies will
change as each young person plays with a super-8 mm
camera, as each college student graduates from film studies
courses, and as each new director begins his first film. As
long as movies are being made they will continue to reflect
our changing culture.

THE
MOVIES

○○○○○○○○○○○○○○○○○○○○○○○○○○○○○

PRODUCTION

MOVIE-MAKING: THE COLLABORATIVE ART

The history of the movies began with individual inventors, but it was carried forward through the years by teamwork. Very few movies have been made by one person alone; those that have are generally labelled as experimental films, and it is not possible to discuss them in the limited space here. Most movies are made through the collaborative efforts of dozens, and sometimes hundreds, of artists and technicians. However, the emphasis in the first part of this book would suggest that the history of the movies is really just the history of the efforts of great directors—Griffith, Eisenstein, Flaherty, Renoir, Welles, Ford, Fellini, and others. After all, they were the people who discovered the unique elements of the art, developed the techniques, and conceived new and more original ways of expressing themselves with it.

For some viewers and critics, the director *is* the most important person in the making of a film—the source of its vision, its energy, and its final form. This view of the director's role originated in France in the early 1950s as the *auteur* theory, which means, quite simply, that the director is the "author" of the film. Basically, this theory values the director as the dominant artistic creator of a film and assumes that his stylistic contributions are more apparent and more important than the contributions made by others working on the same film. As you can imagine, this theory provokes considerable argument between those who place the film director above his collaborators and those who see film as a collaborative art.

The *auteur* theory has been responsible for some of our best film criticism, for its greatest strength is that it asks us to consider the movies seriously. The *auteur* critics ask us to stop thinking of the movies only as entertainment and to place them on the same level as the other arts; they also want us to have fun at the movies. When we think of one of the other arts, such as painting or sculpture, we think of the painter or the sculptor; in the same way, we should think of the film director when we consider the film.

If we accept the *auteur* approach to the movies, then we can easily discuss a "Robert Flaherty film" or a "John Ford film." Each of these directors shapes his raw material according to his personal vision, a vision which is transformed into film by his personal approach to all the other aspects of film-making. If we were to look at the major films of each of these directors, we would see a repetition of certain visual motifs, certain themes, certain conflicts, and even certain actors, actresses, and locations. These distinguishing characteristics would give us a "key" to the director and to his films. As we pick out the central concerns of a director so we define his style as the "author" of his films.

For those interested in this highly personal approach to film-making and film criticism, the *auteur* theory is very useful. But for those interested in all that goes on before a movie is completed, the *auteur* theory is limited because it neglects the one fact that cannot be neglected. Moviemaking is an act of collaboration that involves many people. Much more than painting or sculpture or literature, it is a mechanical art. Most painters, sculptors, and writers work on a one-to-one basis with their materials; in other words, they tend to work alone, handle their tools themselves, and finish their projects by themselves. The raw materials they use come from a variety of sources, but the actual molding of these things into a work of art is generally the responsibility of the individual artist. The painter deals directly with paint and canvas; the sculptor works directly with clay, wood, metals, or fibers; the writer uses the library for research and puts pen or typewriter to paper to develop his thoughts. But the work of a filmmaker is quite different, no matter how small the project, how personal the approach, or how limited the budget.

Making a film is a complicated artistic and technical process. The filmmaker is dependent upon technology from the moment the raw film stock is purchased, through its exposure, processing, and editing, to the final moment when

the movie is completed and shown to an audience. No matter
how resourceful the filmmaker may be, he or she is always
dependent upon other technicians and craftsmen. And no
matter how clear the filmmaker's idea of the film might be
at the start, that film changes considerably between its early
idea stages and the final print that is released to the public.
Again, the reason for this is the collaborative nature of the
art of film-making. Various members of the production unit
work together to complete the film. Although the director in
most cases may be the source of both first inspiration and
final judgment, he or she would never get very far without
the creative team that supports all movie-making.

The people who work together to make movies are known
as the production unit, whose size varies with the size of
the production. In our discussion here we shall consider
only feature-length fiction films made in conventional studios for theatrical release. We shall not discuss the smaller,
independent productions of other fiction films or of animated or nonfiction films for the simple reason that these
are often made with production units that differ in size and
composition from the standard unit discussed here. When
you understand how the artists and technicians of a major
Hollywood studio work together to make a film, then you
will have no difficulty in understanding how almost any
other type of film is made.

As with most American businesses, the technical side of
the film industry has been dominated by men. Most directors
and cinematographers are men, but women have made important contributions as producers, script writers, editors,
script supervisors, costume designers, and, of course, as
actresses. And in the long history of the major Hollywood
studios there have been several notable women film direc-

tors: Dorothy Arzner, Ruth Ann Baldwin, Mary Ellen Bute, Storm de Hirsch, Ida Lupino, Barbara Loden, Lois Weber, and Elaine May. In Europe there have been more women directors, as well as more women in the film industry. Notable European women film directors include, in Russia, Esther Shub; in Germany, Leni Riefenstahl; in Sweden, Mai Zetterling; in Italy, Liliana Cavani and Lina Wertmüller; in Great Britain, Joy Batchelor and Muriel Box; in France, Jacqueline Audry, Germaine Dulac, Marguerite Duras, Alice Guy, Agnes Varda; and in Canada, Joyce Wieland. American women have been more successful in independent nonfiction and experimental film production than in Hollywood; important films have been made by Susan Sontag, Marie Menken, Maya Deren, Shirley Clarke, Martha Coolidge, and Helen van Dongen.

THE PRODUCTION UNIT

The production unit for a feature-length film made by a studio (either on sound stages or on location, or both) includes the following basic personnel: producer, production manager, director, script writer, script supervisor, cinematographer, actors and actresses, camera operator, editor, art director, set designer, costume designer, musical composer, make-up artist, hairdresser, and various technical supervisors of such elements as lighting, sound recording, and special effects. Each of these key people has one or more assistants, and the entire unit is, in turn, supported by a crew of secretaries, managers and assistant managers, technicians and, depending upon the production, such specialized people as extras for crowd scenes and experts to

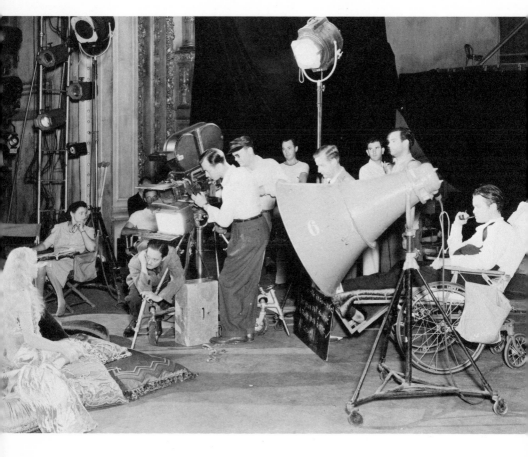

Production Unit: Preparing to shoot a scene for *Citizen Kane* are actress Dorothy Comingore (on cushions), the script supervisor (seated in chair), cinematographer Gregg Toland (beneath camera), camera operator, various lighting and sound assistants, and director Orson Welles (in wheelchair).

perform dangerous stunts. Because movie-making is complicated and expensive, it requires an efficient unit if the best
results are to be obtained. The following section will explain
in brief the specific functions of the basic personnel of a
typical movie production unit.

◉ *Producer* ◉

The producer is chiefly concerned with the business side of
movie-making, but since the producer often owns all or part
of the project being filmed, or is directly responsible to the
studio which does own it, he is more than just a person responsible for the facts and figures. The producer is involved
in all aspects of production from the choosing and writing
of the script, through the actual filming, to the distribution
and promotion of the completed film. The producer controls
all the personnel in the production unit, including the director, but he ordinarily leaves artistic decisions to those best
qualified and responsible for them. However, in Hollywood
history there have been some highly gifted producers, including Irving Thalberg, Sidney Franklin, Arthur Freed,
Joseph L. Mankiewicz, David O. Selznick, Darryl Zanuck,
Pandro Berman, Merian C. Cooper, and Dore Schary. The
producer has the power to step in, take over, and make decisions when costs are running above budget, when the progress of the film is behind schedule, or when he (or the
studio) feels that the completed film will not be a success
with the public.

The role of the producer, therefore, is not an easy one, nor
is it easy for directors, actors, or other artists to understand

a producer's power. As the industry developed the function and importance of the producer increased; as films became more expensive control over them became more necessary to protect the investments of those who had financed them. In some ways a producer is similar to the manager of the manufacturing plant. He keeps an eye on production, delivers the product on schedule, hires and fires employees (presumably on the basis of their merit), and takes final responsibility for what his team has made. But the producer's title is misleading, for he does not actually produce anything so much as he supervises those who do.

The producer works closely in the selection of actors and actresses, and he makes sure that the length of their contracts fits the overall shooting schedule. He goes over the shooting script (the screenplay broken down into shots, scenes, and locations) to plan indoor sound-stage settings and outdoor shooting locations. The locations must be scouted for such all-important variables as weather, geography, local facilities, transportation, and accessibility. The shooting schedule must be planned around another set of variables, which includes shooting "out of continuity" (in other words, a film in which the last scene might be shot before the first) and weather (when the script calls for sun, the schedule must be planned for a time of year when the sun is likely to shine). When the movie is completed, the producer is in charge of selling it to distributors, of planning advertising and publicity, and of other agreements, such as sales to television. If the film is successful at the box office, the producer takes a large share of the profits; if it wins awards, such as the Academy Award Oscar for the best picture, it is the producer, not the director, who receives it.

◑ *Director* ◑

In a motion picture studio the producer takes care of the business while the director takes care of the art of making a film. Basically, the director's task is to interpret the script and transfer it to the screen. His relationship to the film project and to the production unit, both before and during shooting, can vary widely from almost no participation in choosing and writing the script to the closest possible collaboration. In some productions of the major Hollywood studios directors were assigned to projects in one week and expected to begin work in the next. In others the director was involved from the very beginning and participated in the choice of script, writer, cast, and other key personnel, as well as the locations and such elements as design and costumes.

But no matter what assistance he might have or to what extent he may be involved, the director usually bears the artistic responsibility for the success or failure of a movie. When the film is financially successful or wins an Academy Award Oscar, the producer will take a large share of the credit; when the film is not successful, the director is often given the major share of the blame. As noted before, the size of the production unit depends on the size of the project being filmed. If it is a large project, the director will most often have an assistant director whose functions include supervision of second-unit shooting (production located away from the main set or studio), maintenance of communication between producer and director, and maintenance of budgets and shooting schedules.

One of the director's main jobs is setting and maintain-

Director Charlie Chaplin seated behind the cameras
on the set of *The Gold Rush.*

ing the overall defining quality of the film. The French
auteur theorists call this *mise-en-scène*, literally the "putting on of the scene." This includes the settings, the movements of the actors in relation to the settings, the lighting,
and overall design and composition of the photographic
images, the sound recording, and other details which affect
the "look" or "feel" of the film.

Another important job is evoking successful performances
from the actors and actresses in the film. Some performers
require little direction; others have to be taken step by step
through each scene. In either case the working relationship
between the director and the cast is a very important one.

When there are stars in the cast, this relationship may change. Some stars are temperamental and difficult to work with; others are thoroughly professional and are easy to work with. At the same time, some directors can be temperamental and make it difficult for the actors to work with them. But the quality of the film depends on the director's working techniques, on his ability to tell his crew what he wants, on his adaptability to the actors' needs, and on his talent to evoke performances from them which will make the film what it is supposed to be.

Together the director and the producer make the important decisions about script, cast, editing, set and costume design, music, and photography. These two people are most responsible for the success or failure of any movie, but they would never accomplish anything without the other members of the production unit.

◑ Script Writer ◑

The script writer is responsible for the script of the film, whether the story is original or adapted from another source, such as a play or novel. The script writer works closely with the producer and director, but his or her control over the final script varies greatly.

The development of a script covers several stages. In its earliest form a script may be called a synopsis, in which the essential ideas and structure for the film are briefly described. This synopsis is discussed and developed in sessions known as story conferences, during which it is transformed from an outline into what is known as a rough draft screenplay (or scenario). These story conferences usually involve the writer, the director, and the producer; when the time comes to discuss actual production, this group is enlarged to include the production manager, the director of photography, the designer of sets and costumes, and other important technicians. Their purpose in discussing the script together is to formulate a shooting script (one in which each scene and shot is detailed to include technical information about such elements as photography). Finally, when the film has been edited and is ready for distribution, a cutting-continuity script is prepared; this specialized script includes the number, kind, and duration of shots, the kind of transitions, the exact dialogue, and the sound effects.

The shooting script is one of the most important elements in the making of a movie. Before the movie comes to life on the screen, it must first be expressed on paper, although many directors rely very little on detailed shooting scripts. Some directors prefer to stick closely to a carefully detailed script, while others prefer to improvise as they go along. In either case changes often occur between the printed and the filmed version of a script. But the shooting script serves as an invaluable guide to all members of the production unit, for it indicates where everything *ought* to be. The director and others have the opportunity to change things as they go along, but the shooting script provides a guide and a reference point.

Although we tend to think of movies in *visual* terms, we should also remember the *verbal* elements that create the characters, develop the plot, and contain the dialogue. Some directors, such as Ingmar Bergman, write their own scripts; others, such as Stanley Kubrick, collaborate with other writers (with Arthur Clarke on *2001: A Space Odyssey*) or adapt the work of other writers (Kubrick adapted Thackeray's novel for *Barry Lyndon* and Anthony Burgess's novel for *A Clockwork Orange*). The writer's job does not end when production begins; the script may be changed and reworked many times, but if the idea of a writer's script is good, it will never be lost. The script writer functions as a crucial link between the director and the actors and is the key to many of the masterpieces of movie history.

◉ *Cinematographer* ◉

Movie photography is the responsibility of two people: the director of photography and the camera operator. The director of photography (also called the cinematographer) attends the story conferences and plans the shots to be filmed in consultation with the director, writer, and other members of the unit. The camera operator is the person responsible for overseeing the lighting and operating the camera used in shooting the film. In many films the two roles are performed by the same person (who shall be called the cinematographer here).

As we have seen, the writer is the direct link between the director and the actors, for his script provides the plot and dialogue which the actors perform. The persons responsible for photography provide another link between the director and the technology that must be adapted and controlled in the shooting of a film. The earliest moviemaker was all things in one; he was writer, producer, director, camera operator, designer, technician, editor, and often actor as well. But as the film industry became more specialized, each of these functions was assigned to a professional in the field. And no member of the unit is more specialized in his field than the cinematographer.

Movie-making combines many arts, and the final product is a sum of these contributions, but a great part of a film's impact is its visual appearance. The cinematographer is ultimately responsible for the way a film appears on the screen. From the earliest days of movie history various cinematographers have made a significant contribution to the development of cinematic style. They have introduced new methods of lighting, new types of shots, and new techniques of composition. The flattering appearance of many stars on the screen results from the attention of their favorite cinematographers. Both in black-and-white and color cinematography, these artists have shaped the direction of movie history. Today it is the artists in sound recording who are making the major progress, but the contribution of the cinematographers continues to be of paramount importance.

In the simplest terms, the cinematographer translates the director's vision into something the audience can also see. In the ideal production unit the cinematographer thinks along with the director. Just as the script writer is responsible for the verbal elements of plot and dialogue, the cinematographer must in part account for a film's visual look. And basic to the decisions he makes is the matter of what his lens will see. The camera lens is not a human eye, for it is more accurate and less selective. The cinematographer is concerned with many things, but most important is the overall composition of each shot. Composition is the arrangement of the scene to be filmed, as well as the appearance of the scene on the screen, and it involves matters of height, width, depth, lighting, and, of course, placement of people and objects. In addition, the cinematographer must know all about such technical matters as choice of film stock, camera lenses, and the various conveyances which help a camera to move, such as cranes, booms, and dollies.

Later in this section we shall examine some of the techniques and equipment that are used in movie-making. That specific technology is what makes the movies possible; without the professional artists and technicians who operate this equipment, movies could never be made. Of this group of men and women behind the scenes no one is more important than the cinematographer. He and his camera help express the director's vision in photographic images.

◎ Designs, Costumes, Make-Up ◎

Giving life to a movie idea is a complex process. It begins as early as the story conferences and continues through shooting and editing. It involves the people we have been discussing: the producer, director, writer, and cinematographer. But it also involves the art director, the person responsible for designing and overseeing the construction of sets for a studio film. Along with the cinematographer the art director is responsible for the overall visual style of a film. On location shooting the art director chooses the natural sets so that they will blend with footage shot in the studio.

The art director often supervises the designer of the sets (or set decorator) and the designer of the costumes. The designer-decorator is in charge of choosing furniture and accessories, while the costume designer creates the clothes worn by the actors. These professionals must be familiar with various historical styles in decor and costume, and they are ultimately responsible for helping the art director to visualize a film. The heavy lighting on most sets requires

Director Mervyn LeRoy (center) studies a model
of the staircase set designed by art director Anton Grot
(left) for the dance numbers staged by choreographer
Busby Berkeley (right) for *Golddiggers of 1933*.

The set as seen in the film.

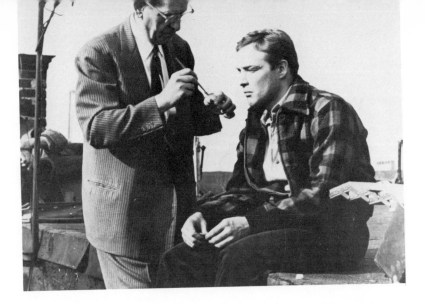

Above: A make-up artist gives Marlon Brando the appearance of an eye injury for a scene in Elia Kazan's *On the Waterfront* (1954).

Below: Costumes play a vital part in establishing the period in such films as *Jezebel* (1938), starring Bette Davis.

that actors and actresses wear make-up to insure an appearance that is consistent with the overall look of the film. The intensity of studio lighting can bring out the best and the worst in a person's appearance, and the make-up artist is there to insure that the best is what the audience sees. This can be an easy or a challenging task, depending upon the nature of the movie, and ranges from the application of ordinary make-up to the creation of special effects of face and figure. The make-up artist (sometimes called the cosmetician) is a magician in transforming young actresses into old women and older actors into even older monsters.

◐ *Actors and Actresses* ◐

Most of us want to know who is in a movie before we go to see it. We may not be familiar with the director, and we probably don't pay too much attention to the names of the cinematographer or art director, but we want to know the names of the actors and actresses. The business of making movies is also the business of creating movie stars.

The people who play the various parts in movies can be separated into certain categories, depending upon their own importance or the importance of the role they play. A star is a person who has become famous for playing leading roles in popular films; this person may or may not be a "type" (in other words, someone who plays the same sort of part in every film, such as a romantic singer or a cowboy), but, in any case, a star's name is often as important as the name of the film and is often the reason the audience pays to see the film in the first place.

Movie actors are sometimes the least specialized members

Ingrid Thulin and Liv Ullmann, seen in close-up,
in Ingmar Bergman's *Cries and Whispers* (1973).

of the production unit. Some of them have so little formal training as actors that audiences would laugh them off the stage of a theater; however, these same people are often screen stars of great popularity.

Movie acting is very different from stage acting, and the results are also different. The image of the movie actor appears on the screen many times the actual size of the person who appears on the stage. His every movement, every utterance, every gesture, is controlled by the technicians behind the camera, in the recording booth, and at the editing table; these people can transform his performance in any way they wish. The stage actor or actress is either in full view of the audience or partially hidden or off-stage altogether; the audience either hears that person clearly or they don't hear him at all, but his impact on them is almost always his own responsibility, not the responsibility of craftsmen and technicians operating complicated equipment. A movie is made in bits and pieces, shot by shot, scene by scene, but not necessarily in the order that those pieces will be seen on the screen. Depending upon such factors as the shooting schedule, the weather, and the mood and the availability of the cast, a movie may be shot from beginning to end, from end to beginning, or in some random fashion that satisfies the shooting schedule and eventually comes to an end. Among other things this requires the actors and actresses to be very flexible and patient. But stage actors do not have this problem, even though their work may be more difficult in other ways, for a stage actor learns his part and performs it in the same way each night.

Good acting is not easy to define for it often relies on the interplay of several factors. Sometimes a good performance is the result of a particular actor's training in the art or skill at portraying a particular type of role or just professional versatility. At other times the director encourages a particular performance from an actor. And at still other times it results not so much from what the actors do but from the nature of the characters they are playing. For example, in a film based on one of the stories about James Bond we expect the actor who plays James Bond (and there have been several) to "act like" the James Bond we imagine from reading the books; it is the character, not the particular actor, who is important here.

Some actors and actresses are famous for their low-keyed approach to roles; others are popular because they overact (or "chew up the scenery," as such a performance is known). Some are famous for their singing (Elvis Presley), swimming (Esther Williams), or dancing (Fred Astaire). And still others (like Henry Fonda) have become stars for their association with certain historical persons whose lives they have portrayed. And some (like Katharine Hepburn) are popular for the simple reason that they perform year after year, in movie after movie, and always give a good performance. There are no rules and no easy answers in the subject of acting.

Some actors and actresses succeed because they can act, some because they are beautiful, some because they are smart, and some because they are all of these things. However, the main key to the success of an actor or actress is the audience, for traditionally the audience supports the stars it likes. There are signs that audiences now are seeking out directors or stories or even changing their moviegoing habits according to the opinions of critics. But over the years the major Hollywood studios transformed actors or actresses into stars. The star system consists of putting an actor in a few good roles, promoting him and the film with constant publicity in newspapers and fan magazines and on television, and then repeating this pattern when success has been achieved. It is based, quite simply, on giving the public what it wants or what it thinks it wants or what the studios say it wants.

But stars are not the only people on the screen, and the basic roles for actors and actresses include the following:

BIT PART.   A minor but distinguishable role.

CHARACTER PART.   An actor or actress who specializes in playing well-defined types, such as society ladies, butlers, gamblers, or pompous bankers.

HEAVY.   The villain or "bad guy" and a typical character part. The name comes from the fact that early screen villains were often fat or heavy men. Peter Lorre and Sydney Greenstreet are classic examples of heavies.

INGÉNUE.   The role of an innocent or inexperienced young woman. In her early pictures Judy Garland was an ingénue.

JUVENILE.   The role of an innocent or inexperienced young man or woman, usually a child actor or actress, such as Shirley Temple or Mickey Rooney.

ROMANTIC LEADS.   The main or most important character in a love story or musical picture. Gary Cooper and Marlene Dietrich are famous romantic leads.

121

One of the screen's great romantic teams: Vivien
Leigh (as Scarlett O'Hara) and Clark Gable (as Rhett
Butler) in Victor Fleming's *Gone with the Wind* (1939).

ROMANTIC TEAMS. Actors and actresses famous for costarring as couples in love stories of musical pictures. Examples include Fred Astaire and Ginger Rogers, Jeanette MacDonald and Nelson Eddy, and Roy Rogers and Dale Evans.

SIDEKICK. The constant companion of an actor or actress, usually a humorous character and frequently played by a character actor. In the many Roy Rogers–Dale Evans films George "Gabby" Hayes played the sidekick to Roy Rogers; in *Gone with the Wind* Butterfly McQueen played the companion to Vivien Leigh.

STAND-IN. The look alike for an actor or actress who duplicates the actor's movements to enable lighting and camera movements to be arranged before the actual shooting of a picture. The stand-in is employed only for the most important stars, but even animal stars like Lassie have had stand-ins.

EXTRA. A performer usually hired by the day to play a minor part, usually in a crowd or mob scene. The extra does not speak, except in a crowd scene, for speaking means acting (in terms of contracts by which actors are employed). Extras are paid low wages, in contrast to most actors and actresses, but many of them are professionals who have worked for years, mostly for the excitement and pleasure of being involved in making movies.

◑ *Editor* ◑

The editor is the artist responsible for the process of assembling a movie from the pieces of film and sound track which have been shot and recorded. On some films the supervising editor is responsible for the overall task of editing; in this case he or she plays a central role in determining the length, arrangement, and rhythm of the shots to be included in the film. Often the actual work is done by an editor (or cutter) whose primary responsibility is the mechanical labor involved in cutting, trimming, and splicing the pieces of film together.

Editing, like writing, is a solitary task requiring patience and a clear sense of the nature of the film. The editor selects and arranges various shots and then, guided by various principles, gives rhythm to these shots by joining them together. The editor may work simply from the beginning of the story to the end, joining scene after scene in a straightforward manner. He may startle his viewers by creating relationships between scenes that are not inherent in them, or he may rearrange time by using the familiar flashback (in which we see some action or scene previous to the present time sequence of the film) or the flash-forward (which presents some action or scene which occurs after the present time of the film). He may match two photographic images to create a transition between one scene and another, or he may order the processing laboratory to provide such technical effects as dissolves, fade-outs, or fade-ins.

The editing of a film is closely related to all aspects of its production. Some directors work from a shooting script that is so carefully detailed that the editor's job becomes merely one of assembling prearranged pieces. Other directors will shoot a particular scene from several camera angles and leave it up to the editor to choose the one which best fits the look of the film. Still other directors deliver such a confused mess of footage to the editor that his or her function is to create order out of chaos. The role of an

Editor Helen van Dongen at work on Robert Flaherty's *Louisiana Story* (1948).

editor is as difficult to define as the role of a director or writer. When all members of the production unit understand the idea of a film, and when all of them work together, sharing ideas and proceeding toward a common goal, then the responsibility of each of them is increased. Some editors are little more than technicians; others are great artists who help a director to clarify his thoughts.

The power of a movie is in its movement. As the Russian Eisenstein recognized in the late 1920s, it is editing which makes a movie *move* the way the director wants it to move. Long after the film has been shot, the editor sits alone with the footage, deciding what to include, what to leave out, and the pace at which it will eventually move on the screen. The editor has a special, direct contact with the film, a contact that is his or hers alone.

◑ *Sound Recorder* ◑

Sound recording involves several experts: (1) a chief technician in charge of all matters of recording; (2) a mixer responsible for mixing or combining several separate sound tracks into one sound track; (3) technicians who secure, wire, and set up microphones, lay cables, operate the tape recording machines, and move the microphones which travel on booms (a boom is a mobile arm which travels above and out of sight of the camera).

◑ *Musical Composer or Arranger* ◑

The person responsible for the musical score may compose his own original material or adapt the material of another composer. In the films discussed at the conclusion of this

126

book, Virgil Thomson wrote the original score for *Louisiana Story*, while Alfred Newman arranged familiar folk melodies as well as his own material for *The Grapes of Wrath*. The composer-arranger may work with the director during the shooting of the film—the best way to get the feel of the film while it is being shot—or he may compose a score after the film has been shot and edited—the usual manner in which it is done. Some directors rely on the musical score, and others use only small bits of recorded music available in studio music libraries. Often a theme song is added to the score; if it becomes popular or wins an Academy Award, it is an important factor in helping to promote the film.

◑ Script Supervisor ◑

The script supervisor makes certain that the director follows the shooting script to insure that there are no discrepancies between shots. For example, it is the script supervisor's task to make notes on camera position, lighting, and placement of actors so that one shot will match another if they are in a consecutive sequence. If there are three shots in a sequence, and the characters are smoking cigarettes in the first shot, then the script supervisor notes this so that they will be provided with cigarettes when the shooting resumes for the second shot.

◑ Special Effects Experts ◑

When you see a film like *Earthquake* (1975) or *Towering Inferno* (1974), you are seeing the work of special effects experts. These artists work with various laboratories to create optical effects (optical illusions) or with miniature sets to re-create a scene that would be impossible to stage in life-size proportions. They can blow up bridges, transform men into animals, or create giant dinosaurs. They can transform fleets of toy boats into a powerful navy, and they are largely responsible for the great success of the "disaster" movies of recent years. But special effects experts have also made possible such different films as *King Kong* (1933) and *Citizen Kane* (1941).

The work of special effects experts is not limited to visual trickery, for they create special sound effects also. (The coming of sound created the need for special sound effects —in other words, those that were not "naturally" part of the sound being recorded—but these are too complicated to be discussed in this introductory book.) Today there are three different ways in which special visual effects are achieved: (1) in the camera, (2) in the laboratory where the film is processed, (3) a combination of both. Camera trickery takes advantage of the fact that all sorts of interruptions may take place while a film is being shot. A camera can fool the eye in a variety of ways, and most of us are so familiar with movies that we do not stop to question the things that the camera gets away with. In other words, we have been tricked so many times that we do not really know where the trickery begins and ends. Laboratory trickery is performed for the most part on a machine called the optical printer, which can handle almost any optical effect specified by the experts, including fades, dissolves, wipes, superimpositions, and a variety of distortions.

◐ *Stunt Performers* ◐

When Robert Redford gets into a fight in *Butch Cassidy and the Sundance Kid* (1969), the chances are that he is not in the fight at all but that a "double" is performing for him. Stunt performers act as doubles for actors and actresses when the action called for in the script is dangerous. Other stunt performers are experts at various sports or at driving fast cars or at falling off horses without getting hurt. Great skill is used in photographing these performers so that the audience sees their work but not their faces; when the film is edited, we are fooled into thinking that the stars of a picture are also excellent skiers or boxers or motorcyclists. François Truffaut's delightful film *Day for Night* (1973) shows many of the behind-the-scenes activities of special effects experts, stunt performers, and other movie magicians.

◐ *Supporting Crew* ◐

In addition to the professionals in any basic production unit there are still others who work in various capacities to assist them. These include grips, whose main function is to move scenery, lights, and equipment; properties staff, whose task it is to obtain and maintain the various props used on the sets; dance and vocal coaches, who train and rehearse dancers and singers; voice coaches, who help actors and actresses learn different dialects or voices; hairdressers; costume and make-up assistants; musical staff, including orchestra;

carpenters and workmen who build scenery; and technical advisers who are hired to advise the directors or actors on special matters, such as fencing, Oriental dance, or medieval costumes.

THE STUDIO AND EQUIPMENT

From 1930 to 1950 the major Hollywood studios were great factories with an almost endless capability to create anything a director wanted. Their carpentry shops and workrooms could fabricate furniture, decorations, and settings of any period in world history, and their costume departments could design and create appropriate costumes. The giant sound stages could be filled with almost anything from mountain peaks to huge tanks of water on which ships could engage in combat. On the vast open-air back lots whole city streets or villages could be built, perfect down to the last detail—except that it was usually only the fronts of buildings that were completed, since the interiors were built inside on sound stages. When the appropriate sets could not be built, the studio location experts would travel around the world to find the perfect spot in which to house a production and make a film or part of a film. In those fabulous days, when the studios were called ''dream factories,'' nothing stood in the way of making movies. It is still possible, of course, to make movies that are as elaborate as those made in the Hollywood studios, but now that most of those studios and their great resources have disappeared, the work must be done independently and at a far greater cost. For this reason major film productions that involve elaborate settings are often produced in foreign countries; in the United

States labor unions, expensive materials, and the absence of major studios make large film production an extremely expensive industry.

In addition to using the skills of many highly trained people, making movies is also a technological process involving many pieces of highly specialized equipment. Although the motion picture camera is the most obvious piece of equipment, there are dozens of other items involved in taking pictures, recording sounds, providing illumination, and helping to move all this equipment around the set, whether it is on an indoor sound stage or outdoors on location. Much of this equipment is far too technical to be discussed in detail in a book of this kind, but a brief introduction to some of it will help to acquaint the reader with the machines that help to make the movies.

◎ Camera Equipment ◎

A motion picture camera is a device for capturing photographic images on motion picture film. The major movie studios use a sound camera, one whose mechanism runs silently to avoid making camera noise which might be picked up by the sound recording equipment. The sound camera is used in shooting sound movies when pictures and sound are being captured simultaneously. Other types of studio cameras include the animation camera (mounted on an animation stand and used for shooting animated films a single frame at a time), the field camera (a relatively portable, lightweight camera used for shooting scenes outside where the sound camera would be too large and awkward to move easily), and the hand camera (a battery-operated or spring-driven field camera which can be carried in the hand and which is used for close, intimate coverage of scenes).

The sound camera is electrically driven and can shoot either 16 mm or 35 mm picture film. Almost all major films are shot in 35 mm and projected in that gauge (width) in major theaters, but, as already noted, 16 mm prints are made for showing in schools, libraries, smaller theaters, homes, and other places where professional equipment and operators are not available or are too expensive to maintain. Projection with 35 mm equipment is costly, requires union operators, and must be covered by expensive fire insurance protection. For the effect of slow-motion photography the shooting is done at high camera speeds, but the film is projected at the regular sound speed of 24 frames per second. When the filming is done at slow camera speed, but projected at regular speed, the viewer sees fast motion. Special effects can be obtained inside the camera. These include stop-motion photography, in which the camera is stopped while the scene is changed, producing the familiar effect of a photograph "coming to life," and reverse-motion photography, where action is shown in reverse sequence. Time-lapse photography is used to record in a few seconds something that happens over a much longer period of time, such as the blossoming of a flower from bud to petals. Frame freezing involves the repetition of a single frame a number of times so that all motion is eliminated.

The cinematographer is concerned with composition; in other words, with the way a scene looks within the borders of the frame of the viewfinder of his camera, and thus the way it will appear on the screen. But since the camera frequently moves, he must also be concerned with composition that is constantly changing. The most familiar ways of

132

moving the camera are tilting (the camera moves up and down on a vertical axis), panning (the camera moves along a horizontal plane), tracking (the camera moves toward or away from a fixed object, or it moves with a moving object at the same or different speed), and booming or craning (mounted on a boom or crane so that it moves upward from or downward toward the object). The development of the zoom lens has made possible the technique known as zooming, which creates the effect of camera movement toward or away from a person or object without actually moving the camera; the lens itself moves and automatically focuses itself. A moving camera can transform composition and make it continually exciting, but shots taken from a stationary camera are equally exciting. What is important is that any movement of the camera be appropriate to the subject and mood of the film.

The smallest component of any movie is the shot (a section of film that has been exposed without interrupting one single running of the camera). The editor combines shots into scenes, and scenes into sequences, and sequences into the completed film. A scene is a group of shots in which the action is continuous; this action may include flashbacks or flash-forwards, but the basic narrative action is continuous. A sequence is a group of scenes (but may also be a group of shots) which together form a basic narrative unit in a film script. A shot is categorized by three things: (1) the distance between the camera and the person or object being filmed, (2) the angle of the camera in relation to the person or object, (3) the content (or composition) of what is being filmed. The four most common shots of people are: (1) the long shot, in which the subject is seen in full length; (2) the medium shot, in which the subject is seen from the knees upward; (3) the close shot, in which the subject is seen from the shoulders upward; and (4) the close-up, in which the subject's head occupies the full frame; the extreme close-up shot includes only one part of the face. The camera can be positioned at almost any angle in relation to the person or object being filmed, but the most common angles are (1) the low angle, in which the camera is positioned below the subject; (2) the high angle, in which the camera is above the subject; and (3) the eye level, in which the camera is positioned at the eye level of the subject. In addition to the kinds of shots mentioned above (long, medium, and close-up) there are dolly, follow, tracking, or trucking shots in which the camera is in motion on a dolly or truck; it can move in closer to the subject or follow it as it moves.

The cinematographer must choose each shot, and for each shot he must choose the appropriate lens for his camera. Since the kind of film stock has been chosen in advance, he must keep its particular properties in mind while choosing shots and lenses. Different decisions must be made for color photography and for black-and-white photography, for indoor and outdoor photography, and for movies being shot with natural or artificial light. There are as many kinds of lenses as there are kinds of film stock and ways of lighting a scene. The cinematographer decides which to use, guided by his education, experience, and, in some cases, his experimentation.

From time to time the cinematographer is presented with new lenses, new film stocks, new lighting equipment, new processing methods, and new projection systems. All of this affects the way he sees a scene, the way he composes it, the way he shoots it, and, finally, the way an audience sees it. Some of the most innovative developments in movie history have been made by cinematographers who were told that a certain effect could not be achieved with standard procedures, and who then went on to achieve it by breaking the rules and trying something in a new way. The startling look of Orson Welles's *Citizen Kane* owes much to the imagination and experimentation of Gregg Toland, the cinematographer. Photography is an art as well as a science, and the creative intuition of the cinematographer is every bit as important as the technical properties of his equipment.

A film like Kubrick's *Barry Lyndon* (1975) owes part of its great beauty to the cinematographer. The composition of its color photography is truly breathtaking at times, and many of the scenes recall familiar eighteenth-century French and English paintings. The lighting achieves a major breakthrough in motion picture technology, for special lenses had to be invented to enable the cameras to record scenes that were lit entirely by candles. *Barry Lyndon* is rich in historical details—in sets, costumes, actual locations, make-up, and landscape—and the cinematographer carefully researched the setting so that the lighting, color values, composition, and placement of elements within the frame approximated the look of eighteenth-century Europe.

The first motion picture to use color was D. W. Griffith's *The Birth of a Nation* (1914). Griffith hand-tinted certain sections of the film because color film had not yet been invented. The first and most popular process of color cinematography was patented as Technicolor. The first Technicolor films were shot in the late 1920s, and until the 1950s the Technicolor Corporation monopolized Hollywood production of color films. Technicolor owned the patent to the process, and its technicians had to be present at shootings; it rented the color cameras, it provided the laboratory processing facilities, and it set the standards for color composition. The Technicolor process involves the use of a special camera, the making of three negatives (blue, red, and yellow), and a processing operation which combines these three color values into one print.

The first major improvement after Technicolor was the development in the early 1940s of a class of color film stocks known as integral tripacks. Unlike Technicolor, this stock gathered all three layers of color dye (blue, red, and yellow) into a single emulsion. These stocks were more sensitive to light, provided better definition of color, and, most important, eliminated the need for the special Technicolor camera, consultants, and processing.

◉ *Sound Equipment* ◉

The recording of sound is as important as the photographing of images, but the development of sound has lagged far behind the development of cameras, lenses, stock, and cinematography. Sound recording is the main factor in the sound part of making a sound movie. Today most sound recording is done magnetically on tape; in the 1930s and 1940s it was recorded photographically (or optically) directly on the film alongside the picture image; in the earliest days it was recorded phonographically on a disc.

Magnetic sound recording, the primary recording process throughout the film industry since the 1950s, resembles the familiar home tape-recording unit. Sound waves from a microphone (or a group of microphones) are imprinted (recorded) on a magnetized strip of acetate tape. Its chief advantage over photographic sound recording is improved fidelity; in simple words, magnetic recording *sounds* better than any other kind. Furthermore, magnetic sound-recording equipment is easier to replay and lighter to transport than the other kinds. This portability has been a great advantage to the on-the-spot production of nonfiction films and other types of films where it is necessary to record sound directly.

Sound-recording equipment consists of three basic components: microphones, tape recorders, and mixers. There are several kinds of microphones, but the two most familiar are the directional and nondirectional types. A directional microphone picks up sound from a specific direction and rejects sounds from other directions, while a nondirectional unit picks up sounds from a wide, circular area. Magnetic tape recorders also come in various kinds, but those used most today are for stereophonic recording (sound recorded and reproduced so that it comes, as in real life, from more than one direction). It involves the use of more than one microphone at one time during recording, and the use of two or more loudspeakers when the film is being shown. The sound mixer is a device which electrically (and sometimes electronically) combines and blends the sounds recorded by different microphones. These sounds may have been recorded in different places and at different times, but the mixer can bring them together in one place at one time. Even the simplest sound track involves mixing of such elements as dialogue, music, and sound effects. Modern mixing equipment is making important contributions to the production of sound films; today it is common for a film to have a sound track consisting of sixteen or more separate tracks. Theaters must also be equipped with the most modern projectors and loudspeaker systems if audiences are to hear these sound tracks properly; unfortunately, the conversion of theaters has been slow. Many audiences are unfamiliar with the brilliant quality of new sound films simply because their theaters are not properly equipped to project them.

◒ *Production Equipment* ◒

In professional theaters projectors are usually housed in the projection booth, a small room at the back of the theater. Here the projectionist controls the quality of the picture being shown, as well as the house lights and the sound. Essentially, a projector is the opposite of a camera. Unexposed film stock has passed through a camera, and as the lens opened and closed to admit light images it recorded these images on the film. This exposed film (called a negative) was then processed to become a positive print. This positive print is run through the projector (at 24 frames per second for sound film); a high intensity light strikes it from behind and *projects* each image through a lens onto the screen. The sound track, which runs alongside but ahead of the picture images, passes in front of another lamp; its waves are transmitted through an amplifier into the loudspeakers. In short, a camera *receives* sight and sound images, and a projector *sends* them.

Both sound and silent projectors are classified by the gauge of the film they accommodate. The gauge of a film stock is its width, expressed in the metric measure of millimeters, such as 8 mm, 16 mm, and 35 mm. Film of 8 mm gauge (and super-8 mm) is used most widely for home movies and amateur productions, although there is an increasing use of 8 mm film for experimental film production.

138

Its quality is satisfactory, and it has attracted professionals because 8 mm cameras and projectors are light, inexpensive, and easy to handle. Now it is possible to record sound directly (magnetically) on 8 mm film as it is being run through the camera.

Although the most commonly used professional film is 35 mm, 16 mm is also widely used, especially for productions made on smaller budgets or where the lightweight 16 mm equipment is easier to handle than the relatively heavy and bulky 35 mm equipment. Certain wide-screen processes use various film gauges above 35 mm, the most common of these being 70 mm. Every gauge is compatible with any other gauge. For example, part of a film may be shot in 35 mm and the rest in 16 mm. The cinematographer simply asks the processing laboratory to enlarge the 16 mm film to a 35 mm print; it is also possible to reduce 35 mm film to a 16 mm print. In both cases, though, there is a noticeable loss of quality.

SUMMING UP

When we sit in a theater and watch a movie, we are mostly concerned with the stars and the story. If the movie is good, we tend to forget that it is a movie and think of its stars and its story as real life. At these times we also forget the many people behind the movie on the screen, the members of the production unit who made the movie. But, as we have seen, movie-making is a collaborative art from the moment when an idea for a film is born, to the time when it becomes a business venture, through the entire production process, to the final moment when it is projected before an audience.

Special-effects experts are responsible for scenes like this one from Stanley Kubrick's *2001: A Space Odyssey* (1968).

Countless important people play a role in that collaboration. In fact, it takes more people to make a movie than it does to create any other form of art, and this means a large number of disciplined, trained, and cooperative professionals.

When we are transported, for example, through the fantastic world of Stanley Kubrick's *2001: A Space Odyssey*, we are alone in outer space. It all looks so real that we forget that the space ships are miniatures, that the unexplored terrain has been created by set designers and cinematographers, and that the actors are not really astronauts. When this happens, and it often happens in the movies, then we understand the reason for the teamwork of these many artists. They get credit when their names appear on the screen, but their most satisfying pleasure comes from taking us into their wonderful world and fooling us for a while.

Orson Welles once said, ''Theatre is a collective experience; cinema is the work of one single person.'' Those who support the *auteur* theory would have no problem in agreeing with this, but even though Welles is one of the greatest directors in movie history, it is an extraordinary remark. As we have seen, the making of a movie is an act of collective creativity in which various members of the production unit participate through interaction. They are—in the very best of worlds—following the director and transferring his vision into images of sight and sound. Film-making is more than just conception and directing, for it involves the skills and talents of the actors and actresses, cinematographer, writer, editor, sound recordist, designer, and production crew. One man or woman sitting alone in a room can conceive a film. But an entire crew of specialized artists and technicians stand between that moment of inspiration and the final moment in which the inspiration becomes the reality of a completed film.

Film-making is both an art and an industry, and its success depends upon an interaction, not between artist and businessman, for that turns movies into products and art into a commodity, but between artists and technicians, a true collaboration of trained, gifted professionals dedicated to their art.

THE MOVIES

○○○○○○○○○○○○○○○○○○○○○○○○○○○○○○

CRITICISM

ThinkiNq AbouT film

The final test of a movie is what the members of the audience think and say about it. But what you the viewer say about a movie should depend on what you know about it and how you look at it. In short, criticism depends on the kind of knowledge you have from knowing about movies in general, about the particular movie you are seeing, as well as the kind of knowledge that comes from real-life experience. Inherent taste is as important to good criticism as an informed background. Perception (a keen eye), intuition (a

good guess), and observation (attentive viewing) often produce criticism that is every bit as intelligent and influential
as that produced by scholars and critics who have studied
the movies for years. When most of us go to a movie, we
see it with an open mind, with open eyes and ears, yet most
of us have strong feelings for or against the film just as
soon as we have seen it. We rely on a combination of factors
to influence our opinions and our criticism.

Good criticism appears to be a simple combination of
perception, intuition, observation, information, and taste.
Consider then what happens when the average person sees
a film like Robert Altman's *Nashville* (1975). He or she has
not seen all the movies ever made, does not know all about
film history, and certainly is not familiar with all the changes
that have occurred in such film elements as script, narration,
photography, sound recording, and acting. But that viewer
feels somehow that *Nashville* is different from the other
movies that he or she knows. The viewer might have read a
review of this film and would know that the script was created by the actors working together with the director and
script writer. Looking carefully at the film, he realizes that
its story *seems* more real, more lifelike, than other movies,
and that at times it does not seem like a story at all but like
a television documentary. He might have read that the director wanted his film to combine the fictional and nonfictional
approaches into a different kind of storytelling. The viewer
will notice a certain freedom in the photography, sound recording, and acting. And whether or not he likes the film, he
will leave the theater with the impression that *Nashville*
is different. And there is enough in *Nashville* that is different from, say, *The Birth of a Nation* or *Citizen Kane* or *Easy
Rider* or *Jaws* to make the viewer think about it.

Thinking about film is the first step to criticizing and evaluating it. Some critics get paid for writing the reviews with which we agree or disagree, depending upon our own tastes, but we are all critics every time we go to the movies and tell our family or friends about them. We all recognize that the responsible critic is one who tells us what is good about a movie at the same time that he or she tells us what is wrong with it. When someone asks us about a movie, it is easy enough to say, "It's great!" But it is not so easy to say *why* the film is great and *why* our friends should see it.

Good movie criticism should take into consideration both the negative and positive factors which influence the viewer's opinion. Although criticism is the product of your subjective feelings about a movie, not the objective product of some scientific inquiry, you can be a good critic by remembering to watch a movie carefully, to think about it intelligently, and to make your final assessment a combination of all that you thought was good and bad in the film. And you will be even better prepared if you remember the broad outline of film history and the production teamwork which goes into making a movie.

basic elements of movie criticism

A movie critic's standards are based on taste, knowledge, and guesswork. Sometimes, too, the critic just sets these aside and bases his or her judgment on his feelings about a particular director or actor. But criticism is not always fair; often the critic can be as prejudiced and as stupid as any one else in making evaluations. Most of the time, though, the critic considers the appropriateness and effectiveness of many factors concerning each film.

1. Its place in film history and aesthetic tradition.
2. The director's success or failure in communicating his vision.
3. The type of story (fiction or nonfiction) and the script (narrative, dialogue, conflict, and conclusion).
4. The actors and their acting style.
5. The cinematography, lighting, and sound recording.
6. The look of the film (art direction, sets, costumes).
7. The editing (rhythm, pace, transitions, continuity).
8. The musical score.

There are other factors, too, but these are the main ones.

A film's story is perhaps the most important, for the story determines the type of film, the kind of script, the casting of actors, as well as influencing all the other elements of a production. In this final section, we will cover the two major types of film story—nonfiction and fiction; and then will take a closer look at one film from each category—Robert Flaherty's *Louisiana Story* and John Ford's *The Grapes of Wrath*. Each of these films represents its type, yet each uses elements from the other type. Flaherty's nonfiction film tells a fictional story of his own creation, and Ford's fiction film is based on a historical event as interpreted by a novelist, and it uses some footage which looks as if it were made for a nonfiction film about the same subject.

◉ *Nonfiction Film* ◉

In the simplest terms, the nonfiction film dramatizes a factual rather than a fictional situation. That does not mean that a nonfiction film is any more true than a fiction film but that its subject matter is taken from an actual, rather than an imaginary, situation. The nonfiction film-maker takes every opportunity to treat this actual situation with as much creativity as the subject will permit. Generally, the nonfiction film originates in an immediate social situation: sometimes a problem, sometimes a crisis, sometimes an undramatic and seemingly unimportant person or event. *Louisiana Story* originated in a commission from an oil company to make a film for public relations purposes. A nonfiction film is usually filmed on the actual scene, with the actual people, without sets, costumes, written dialogue, or created sound effects. It tries to re-create the feeling of "being there" with as much fidelity to fact as the situation allows.

The typical nonfiction film is structured in two or three parts, with an introduction and conclusion, and tends to follow a pattern which moves from statement of problem to statement of solution. Even more typically it is shot in black and white, with direct sound recording (or simulated sound), a musical score written especially for the film and conceived as part of a cinematic whole, and, often as not, a spoken narration. Usually it runs for thirty minutes, but some nonfiction films run less, and some are much longer. Leni Riefenstahl's *Olympia* (1938), Marcel Ophuls's *The Sorrow and The Pity* (1971), and Louis Malle's *Phantom India* (1974) all run for more than four hours.

The nonfiction filmmaker can choose from many approaches in making a creative treatment of an actual situation, but two have been most common: the documentary approach and the factual approach. Other approaches include the compilation film, the newsreel, the propaganda film, the educational film, and direct cinema.

149

DOCUMENTARY FILM.   The term "documentary film" is often used incorrectly in place of the term "nonfiction film." The difference is one of degree and of kind. All documentary films are nonfiction films, but not all nonfiction films are made with the documentary approach. Nonfiction is the general category into which documentary and the other approaches fit.

The documentary film was developed by John Grierson and others in England during the 1930s; their films were distinguished by their sociopolitical purpose or what we might call their message. The documentary filmmaker wants to use his films for purposes other than entertainment; he wants to persuade, to influence, and to change his audience. His purpose can be an immediate one—such as the explanation of his country's invasion of another in time of crisis (for example, Harry Watt's *Target for Tonight*, 1941)—or it can be a general one—such as informing an audience about such an unfamiliar subject as sharks (for example, Peter Gimbel's *Blue Water, White Death*, 1972).

The documentary filmmaker does not necessarily value subject over style, but there are times when the need to get the message across takes priority over the medium in which that message is expressed. Finally, the documentary film, as Grierson defined it, is an important part of communications in a democracy. For this reason he hoped that it would not be confused with the propaganda film which, in his view, works in the service of the enemies of democracy. But after the 1930s, when Grierson formulated his definitions, World War II showed us that both sides of the conflict can use films of all sorts to educate, persuade, confuse, or just plain lie. And during that war the United States made more propaganda films than its enemies. Today the line between *documentary* and *propaganda* film is often blurred; the principle of *truth* should be the factor which helps to keep them separated.

FACTUAL FILM. The factual film lacks a specific message. In simple terms, the difference between the factual and the documentary approaches to nonfiction film-making is very similar to the difference between the news and the editorial pages of the newspaper. Documentary films are concerned with facts *and* opinion, and factual films are generally concerned only with the facts. Most of the earliest nonfiction films were factual; they simply recorded an important event without making any particular social, political, moral, or cultural comment. Examples include Dickson's *Fred Ott's Sneeze* (1889), Lumière's *Workers Leaving the Lumière Factory* (1895) and *The Baby's Meal* (1895), and early newsreels of such events as Queen Victoria's funeral, the first Wright flight in France, and the sinking of the Austrian battleship *St. Stephen.*

COMPILATION FILM. Many nonfiction films are made up entirely of material compiled and edited from other sources, such as newsreel archives, documentary and factual footage, and even footage that appears in fictional films. This is a highly advanced technique, for it requires a filmmaker with a wide familiarity with what has already been shot by others, as well as an ability to choose and to edit this material. Notable examples of this technique include Frank Capra's *Why We Fight* series (1943–45) and many television series, such as *The Twentieth Century* (1957–64).

NEWSREEL FILM. Newsreels are almost nonexistent today, but at one time these newspapers of the screen, as they were called, were shown in almost every theater, along with a double bill of feature films, a cartoon, a travelogue, and sometimes even a short film. Newsreel and factual films have much in common, except that the newsreel often takes a light-hearted approach to its subject matter and thus does a certain amount of editorializing. Today the newsreel has been replaced by a more serious approach to broadcasting of news reports and special documentaries on television.

PROPAGANDA FILM. Strictly speaking, a propaganda film is one which attempts to propagate, or spread, an idea. Generally speaking, we regard propaganda films as dangerous weapons used by the enemy, but this is shortsighted, for it neglects the fact that the enemy considers our propaganda films to be equally dangerous. A propaganda film almost always distorts and disfigures its subject matter to the point that it is transformed into what the filmmaker wants. Often its content contains outright lies, based on footage which is so heavily edited that it bears little resemblance to the actual situation being portrayed. The greatest and possibly the most dangerous propaganda film ever made is Leni Riefenstahl's *Triumph of the Will* (1935), a cinematic glorification of Adolf Hitler and the Nazi party.

EDUCATIONAL FILM. Nonfiction educational films are used almost everywhere, from classrooms to the battlefield, to instruct people in almost every imaginable subject. These films are produced by such organizations as public agencies, private industries, colleges, and independent producers. Because their major concern is getting the point across, they are often unconcerned with cinematic style, but when they are produced with care, they can be fascinating as well as educational.

DIRECT CINEMA. Since the 1950s direct cinema has constituted a major break with the nonfiction film-making tradition. This new approach to nonfiction film is the most important innovation since the work of Grierson, Flaherty, Lorentz, and others in the 1930s and 1940s. But those currently working in the field have not yet reached any apparent agreement on how to use the technique. Filmmakers who use direct cinema (which is also called by the French term *cinéma vérité*—"film truth") use lightweight equipment in an informal attempt to break down the barriers between filmmaker and subject, to simplify procedure to get at the whole truth and nothing but the truth, and to catch events while they are happening rather than to question events that happened in the past.

Generally, they attempt to capture a carefully selected aspect of reality as directly as possible, with a minimum of obstacles between the filmmaker and his subject. To accomplish this they avoid using scripts, rehearsals, and placing limitations on where the persons in the film may move, what they may say, and where they may say it. The camera work is intimate, often giving the viewer a much more immediate sense that he is there; the sound recording is direct and often clouded by pickup of background noise that lends even more reality; and the editing tends to be continuous rather than discontinuous, striving for a chronological, rather than dramatic, presentation of events. Early important work was done by Richard Leacock, D. A. Pennebaker, William C. Jersey; significant later films are by David and Albert Maysles (*Salesman*, 1969; *Gimme Shelter*, 1970; and *Grey Gardens*, 1976), Michael Wadleigh (*Woodstock*, 1970), and the outstanding films of Frederick Wiseman (including *High School*, 1968; *Hospital*, 1969; *Basic Training*, 1971; *Juvenile Court*, 1973; *Primate*, 1974; and *Welfare*, 1975).

◐ *Fiction Film* ◐

Most of this book is about the kinds of movies that are classified as fiction films. When most people think of the movies, they think of story films about invented characters in invented scenes and situations, or of films about real or historical persons in made-up situations or involved with fictional characters. Except in those instances where fictional films use nonfiction techniques (or incorporate nonfiction footage —for example, *All The President's Men*, 1976), fiction films are different in most important ways from nonfiction films. But the more that movies become as "real" as possible, the more the distinction between nonfiction and fiction will blur, and the less important these distinctions will become. A film like Robert Altman's *Nashville* (1975) points the way to the most promising development in the future of film-making: artistic collaboration beyond the traditional limitations which separate the work of the director, scriptwriter, and actors; techniques in photography and sound recording which reflect the influence of "direct cinema"; and a conscious attempt to say something meaningful about social,

154

moral, and cultural problems. In some ways the fiction film is becoming more and more like the nonfiction film in its thematic and technical approaches to realistic subject matter.

Fiction films are made from all kinds of stories, for all kinds of stars, and about all kinds of situations. The kinds of film stories that are possible vary as much as books in a library, and they are limited only by the imaginations of those who create them. There are certain large, recurring themes such as love, death, war, marriage, and fantasy, and each of these can be approached in ways which range from the comic to the tragic, from the most intelligent to the most frivolous, or from the most creative to the most trite. Some films are made for and about particular stars.

For example, John Wayne's image with the public is that of a tough guy. He is almost always cast in the role of a weather-beaten cowboy or a hard-boiled military man or a tough adventurer. He has never appeared in light comedies or in musicals or in gangster films or in thrillers. The public expects a certain type of film when it goes to see John Wayne, and it is good business sense to give that kind of film to the public. Countless stars have been associated with certain kinds of films, and certain studios excel at making certain kinds of films. Films about ice skating or Kung-fu or racing have their own built-in characteristics. Wise and successful directors, stars, and studios do not tamper with these kinds of films. Recently the "disaster" movie has been very popular, and while each big film is about a different sort of disaster—shipwreck, earthquake, or fire—they are almost identical in kind of script, casting, technical effects, and shock value.

The following list is highly selective, but it attempts to

cover the most popular kinds of fiction films with a few outstanding examples of each. Many of these overlap; for example, the adventure film often includes aspects of the historical and biographical films. And the list neglects many kinds of films, including beach-party movies (a favorite of the 1950s), Kung-fu movies, and others.

ADVENTURE.   Scripts of action, suspense, and history make excellent adventure films. They might involve a chase or an escape, an epic account of some great historical or cultural movement, or a melodramatic spy or war story. Westerns are often adventures, especially when they recount the westward movement or the settling of the various states in the Union. Examples include *Mutiny on the Bounty* (1935, remade in 1952), *Northwest Passage* (1940), and *The Bridge on the River Kwai* (1957). *The Sting* (1973) is a comic adventure, involving aspects of the gangster and thriller films as well.

BIOGRAPHY.   The life story of a famous real person; depending upon subject, it may be an adventure or history film as well. Examples include *The Story of Louis Pasteur* (1935), *Dr. Ehrlich's Magic Bullet* (1940), *The Jolson Story* (1946), *Lawrence of Arabia* (1962), *Funny Girl* (1968), and *Funny Lady* (1975). *Citizen Kane* (1941) is a fictionalized biography.

HISTORY.   A film that deals with a historical subject; generally, these films are based on fact, such as *Elizabeth and Essex* (1939) and *The Virgin Queen* (1955)—both about Queen Elizabeth I—but they can also deal with a fictional

Audiences of all ages like *The Wizard of Oz* (1939), Victor Fleming's film starring Jack Haley (Tin Woodsman), Ray Bolger (Scarecrow), Judy Garland (Dorothy), and Bert Lahr (Cowardly Lion).

character involved in events that seem like factual history (*Captain Horatio Hornblower*, 1951).

CHILDREN'S FILMS.   Many Walt Disney features (animated and nonanimated) are produced for audiences of children, although adults often enjoy these films too. Certain classics, such as *The Wizard of Oz* (1939), appeal to audiences of all ages. Children's films are often screen versions of popular children's books.

GANGSTER. A film about the activities of criminals, usually recounting the illegal activities of one major gangster but sometimes a mob of gangsters, often but not always set during Prohibition in the 1920s and early 1930s. Examples include *Little Caesar* (1930), *Scarface* (1932), *Bonnie and Clyde* (1967), and *Thieves Like Us* (1974).

HORROR. A film intended to horrify or terrify the audience. Examples of this highly popular type of film include the many screen versions of the stories of Dracula and Frankenstein, *Dr. Jekyll and Mr. Hyde* (1932), *The Wolf Man* (1940), and *The Exorcist* (1974).

MONSTER. These enormously popular films are most often about the destructive activities of a monster human or animal. Like horror, disaster, and thriller films, they offer the audience an exciting way of escaping everyday life. Examples include *King Kong* (1933) and *Godzilla* (1955).

DISASTER. A relatively new type of film, dealing with catastrophe and widespread human and physical destruction. Examples include *The Poseidon Adventure* (1972), *Towering Inferno* (1974), *Earthquake* (1974), and *The Hindenburg* (1975).

THRILLER. A film whose story focuses on the activities of a detective in solving a mystery or a crime. There have been many famous screen detectives, including Nick and Nora Charles, Sam Spade, and Philip Marlowe. Film examples include *The Thin Man* (1934), *The Maltese Falcon* (1941), and *The Long Goodbye* (1974).

ROMANCE. A movie which tells a love story. It can be comic, like *Bringing Up Baby* (1938), or serious, like *Gone with*

Monster films like the original *King Kong* (1933)
are among the most popular of all fiction films.

Thriller: *The Maltese Falcon* (1941), starring
Humphrey Bogart (as detective Sam Spade) and featuring Peter Lorre, Mary Astor, and Sydney Greenstreet.

the Wind (1939). There have been many romantic films made especially for romantic acting teams such as Spencer Tracy and Katharine Hepburn, Clark Gable and Joan Crawford, Greer Garson and Walter Pidgeon, Rock Hudson and Doris Day, Richard Burton and Elizabeth Taylor, and Ali McGraw and Steve McQueen.

MUSICAL.   A film whose story is constructed around musical sequences. Since the introduction of sound musicals have been among the most popular of all films; to name but a few types, there have been serious musicals, filmed operas and Broadway shows, light and silly musicals, films about singing cowboys, musical biographies, the Busby Berkeley musicals of the 1930s in which spectacular dance routines were the most important element, the Fred Astaire–Ginger Rogers films, the Judy Garland films, the Nelson Eddy–Jeanette MacDonald films, and the Elvis Presley and Beatles films.

SCIENCE FICTION.   A film with a fantastic or futuristic story, often about visits to, or visitors from, another planet. Some science fiction films are also horror films. Examples include *The Thing* (1952), *The Day the Earth Stood Still* (1952), and *The Invasion of the Body Snatchers* (1956). The most ambitious and most beautiful science fiction film of them all is Stanley Kubrick's *2001: A Space Odyssey* (1968).

COMEDY.   Comedies are among the oldest and most popular of all film types, and, as we have seen, they are most often associated with particular comedians: the Marx Brothers, W. C. Fields and Mae West, Charlie Chaplin, Buster Keaton, Laurel and Hardy, Lucille Ball, Red Skelton, Bing

Above: George Cukor's comic drama *Dinner at Eight* (1933) featured Jean Harlow in a classic interpretation of the "dumb-blonde" stereotype.

Left: Gene Kelly in Stanley Donen's comedy-musical *Singin' in the Rain* (1952).

Crosby and Bob Hope, Woody Allen, and Mel Brooks. In turn, each of these comedians specializes in certain types of comedy, such as slapstick, screwball, or chase.

RELIGIOUS. Films based on religious themes have always been a part of the movies, although many of them are merely excuses for producing another spectacular film based loosely on history. Examples include *The Robe* (1953), *The Ten Commandments* (1956), and *The Greatest Story Ever Told* (1964).

LITERARY ADAPTATIONS. Films based on literature rather than on original screenplays. These include screen adaptations of biblical stories, Shakespeare's plays, famous novels, plays, and short stories. Among the countless examples are *Anna Karenina* (1935), *Wuthering Heights* (1939), *The Grapes of Wrath* (1940), *Tom Jones* (1963), *Ulysses* (1967), and *War and Peace* (American version, 1955; Russian version, 1967).

WAR. A film in which the main action or the focus of the main action is warfare. Many war films are merely another form of adventure film, while others are antiwar in intention. Examples include *All Quiet on the Western Front* (1930), *Grand Illusion* (1937), *The Best Years of Our Lives* (1946), and *The Longest Day* (1962).

WESTERN. Westerns, musicals, and comedies are the staple of the movie industry. Westerns are set anywhere in the American West and present conflicts between the law and outlaws in which the good guys almost always win. There are many celebrated western stars, including Hopalong Cassidy, Tom Mix, Roy Rogers, Gene Autry, Gary Cooper,

Warren Beatty and Julie Christie listen to direction from Robert Altman (right) for his *McCabe & Mrs.
Miller* (1972), a film that is both in and out of the tradition of Hollywood westerns.

John Wayne, and Clint Eastwood; many celebrated western directors, including John Ford, Howard Hawks, and Henry King; and many famous western films, including *The Great Train Robbery* (1903), *Stagecoach* (1939), *My Darling Clementine* (1946), *Red River* (1948), *The Gunfighter* (1950), and *High Noon* (1952).

ANIMATED. Animated films, also called cartoons, are produced generally for audiences of children; they can be short, such as the *Tom and Jerry* or *Roadrunner* series, or full-length, such as *Fantasia* (1940) or *Bambi* (1942). Animation involves a complex process of filming and can often be quite distinguished in its artistry. Its possibilities are not limited to children's films: in the early 1970s Ralph Bakshi's full-length animated features (incorporating live-action sequences) began to appear for adult audiences (*Fritz the Cat, Heavy Traffic*, and *Coonskin*).

EXPERIMENTAL OR UNDERGROUND. Films made by independent filmmakers, often about unfamiliar or unorthodox subjects and often quite innovative in technique. This large field offers many kinds of films made by such important filmmakers as Stan Brakhage, Kenneth Anger, and Andy Warhol. Since many of their films do not tell a story in the conventional sense but deal rather with abstract images, they are a form all to themselves—apart from both the fiction and nonfiction forms.

A CLOSER look AT TWO FILMS

The final section of this book is a close look at two important films: Robert Flaherty's *Louisiana Story* and John Ford's *The Grapes of Wrath*. Since the films are of different kinds, made in different ways, each one needs a different interpretation. The purpose of looking at each film closely is to gain a better understanding of how movies are made and how to evaluate them.

Both Flaherty and Ford were born of Irish parents in the United States, both began their film careers at an early age, and both made important contributions to the development of the American motion picture art. Each in his own way worked outside the film industry, not so much as an opponent of the organized system (Ford, after all, was a Hollywood studio director) but as an individual artist, breaking new ground and establishing new ways in which to make movies. Flaherty made only five films, four of which are considered major landmarks in the development of the nonfiction film. Ford made about 175 films, many of which are regarded as masterpieces of the American fiction film. Flaherty's independently produced nonfiction films are much simpler than Ford's studio-produced movies, but each shows the fine control of a master's hand. Both Flaherty and Ford are *auteurs* of highly personal films which reveal a love of life and people, a respect for traditional humanitarian values, a gift for straightforward storytelling, and, most of all, a passion for telling those stories with a camera.

⊙ *Robert Flaherty and* Louisiana Story *(1948)* ⊙

Robert Flaherty (1884–1951) is the father of the nonfiction film, the first important filmmaker in the world to document real life, using real people with real locations. In his long film-making career, which spanned from 1913 to 1948, he made only five major films, but these insured his reputation as a great storyteller and artist. He had an eye for beauty, a respect for the simple life, and a desire to record these things so that we all might learn. A great deal has been written about him, about his attitude toward primitive cultures, and about his films. But most of this is of secondary importance in contrast to those films. They deserve and merit continual screening, not only for what they say about lands and peoples different from our own but for what they show us about the possibilities of the nonfiction film. At this point in history Flaherty's films might seem old-fashioned, for they are the work of a man who was more content in making simple films about the past rather than dynamic films about the present. But they are gentle films of great beauty, and they speak eloquently for the artistry of their maker.

Flaherty is an *auteur* in every sense of the word, perhaps the first to acknowledge himself as such, for in the credit titles of his second film, *Moana* (1926), Flaherty and his wife Frances are listed as the "authors" of the film. Although Flaherty worked in close collaboration with several other artists (cinematographers, editors, composers), he made his own films and was determined to tell his stories the way he wanted them to be told.

Flaherty was a poet in telling wonderful stories about real places, in creating a lyrical mood in his films, and in avoiding easy answers to the large questions posed by those stories. Each of his films is set in some far-off place: *Nanook of the North* (begun in 1913 and released in 1922) is about Arctic Eskimo life, *Moana* (1926) is about coming of age on a South Seas island, *Man of Aran* (1934) is about the rugged life of the Aran islanders in Ireland, *The Land* (1941) is about the American farmer and his disappearing way of life, and *Louisiana Story* (1948) is about the life of a French-American Cajun boy on the Louisiana bayous. These poetic films help us to transcend the everyday, to explore and even to escape, and finally to understand our own environment with a greater sensitivity to human problems and relationships between man and nature. Flaherty was the first serious artist to make nonfiction films, and what he brought to this new world was his vision of humanity and his enthusiasm for life. He was not a great technician, and the cinematic style of some of his films seems dated to some viewers, but his influence has been enormous.

Flaherty's most famous film is his first, *Nanook of the North*, but his masterpiece is his last, *Louisiana Story*. *Nanook* was a pioneering, independent production, made almost entirely by Flaherty alone; it was financed by a commercial firm, released for theatrical distribution, and became a major success overnight. *Louisiana Story* was a much more ambitious project, involving a large budget, a professional crew, and a different approach. In 1943 Standard Oil offered Flaherty an important and unusual commission for a nonfiction filmmaker; the company would pay all the costs and turn over all the theater revenue to Flaherty for a film which would show the public the long, hard work required to establish an oil-drilling and oil-pumping operation. The film was to be an obvious public relations effort, but Flaherty would have complete artistic control, a budget of $250,000 (a very large sum for a nonfiction film in 1943), and a crew of his own choosing. Flaherty never made another film after *Louisiana Story*, but he never made a finer one before it; if this had been his only film, it alone would have earned him a distinctive reputation.

Louisiana Story was two years in the making and was

the result of the collaborative effort of several outstanding artists. Flaherty was the director, and he wrote the script with his wife, Frances. The editor was Helen van Dongen, a distinguished filmmaker and editor of many famous nonfiction films. The cinematographer was Richard Leacock, who went on to become one of the foremost makers of nonfiction films in the direct cinema method. Both van Dongen and Leacock served as associate producers. The musical score was by the noted American composer Virgil Thomson, and it was recorded by the Philadelphia Orchestra under the direction of Eugene Ormandy. The score is very dramatic in the way it underlines the action and the mood of the film, and while there is some dialogue, the story is revealed mostly through the beautiful images, the well-edited sequences, and the music which conveys so much of what is happening and how the characters feel about it. None of the persons in the film was a professional actor; they were all hired on the spot, although the two main actors—the boy and his father—were chosen from a group which auditioned for the film. The crew also included an associate editor, two persons for music recording, and a miscellaneous supporting crew. Robert Flaherty conceived the idea of the film and he directed it, but it would never have been realized without the close collaboration of these other artists.

Louisiana Story does more than tell the story of how oil is discovered, for it is a Robert Flaherty film, and such an ordinary subject would not have been of great interest to him. Although the film does tell us all we need to know about how an oil well is dug and how the oil is piped to refineries, its principal story is about people and how they are affected by all this activity. Flaherty's attempt to tell these two stories is perhaps a major fault of the film, for while the people are interesting, the story about the oil drilling interferes with Flaherty's attempt to show their lives. Nevertheless, the film does illustrate just how effectively a nonfiction film can both inform and entertain.

The story takes place in a Louisiana bayou where the Cajuns live in close contact with nature. They have simple houses, simple boats, simple clothes, and what appears to be a friendly and fulfilling life. One day this peace is broken by the arrival of a barge which contains a derrick and all the equipment necessary for conducting a drilling operation in search of oil. The story is told through the eyes of a young Cajun boy—Alexander Napoleon Ulysses Latour. He has been named after explorers and conquerors, and he is worthy of the names; much of the film is devoted to his explorations of the beautiful bayous in his little canoe. To a certain extent he also "conquers" this wilderness, for the woods and the bayous are very much his private world. His parents and the men in the oil-drilling crew play minor roles in the film.

The outline of the film is simple. Bayou life is peaceful and quiet; the drilling crew arrives, establishes a successful operation, and leaves. Life is peaceful and quiet again, except that the Latour family now earns a steady income from the oil drilled from their property. Standard Oil is seldom mentioned in the film; the men in the crew are thanked during the opening credits, and brief mention is made of the company in one of the newspaper stories used to explain the drilling process later in the film. But *Louisiana Story* is really no more about oil than *Nanook of the North* is about snow. Basically, the film is about youth, nature, and animals, and the freedom which comes from living close to nature; most of all it is about magic. The boy's world is a supernatural one, full of fantastic spirits that he imagines, and controlled by his belief in the magical properties of his own spit, his bag of salt, and a little frog that he carries inside his shirt. Since we know from the opening sequence that he believes in mermaids and werewolves, it is not surprising that he also believes in this primitive form of magic. He believes in what he sees, and the world of adults seems strange to him, just as his belief in magic seems strange to the adults who observe him. But one adult—Roberty Flaherty—is fascinated by him.

There are five sequences in *Louisiana Story*, and its overall structure is one of great unity. The film moves from peace and quiet to activity and noise, and back again to peace and quiet. It opens and closes with the boy and suggests that his impressions of the natural world will not be changed by the noise and chaos of the industrial world. Of course, Flaherty knew that man's exploration of natural resources was not always this pleasant, and that other men had done much to alter and destroy the ecology of the environment. He knew that innocent people were often trampled in a world devoted to material power, and he knew that industrial giants were rarely generous with their money or benign in their dealings with people. But while he knew these things, he did not relate them to his telling of *Louisiana Story*, for his film is seen through the eyes of a boy whose only friend is a raccoon, and whose closeness to nature is so intense that he will fight an alligator to prove a point.

The first sequence of the film opens slowly and quietly, catching the viewer in a lyrical world of shapes and shadows. In the first scene we see the boy in his canoe floating through a world of bayous, cypress trees, Spanish moss, birds, and

alligators. Leacock's photography is a study in contrasting
images: shimmering light and water for the boy's world of
nature, and solid light and dark for the men's world of
machines. As the boy is about to shoot his gun he hears an
explosion, followed quickly by another; this seems to be
his first awareness of a disturbance in the bayou, something
he does not understand. The images which follow are in-
complete, for they only suggest the size and power of some
anonymous monster; it is not until later, when we see his
father signing a contract with a representative of the oil
company, that we realize that the bayou will never be the
same again. Soon the quiet waters will be shattered by the
roar of speedboats and the incessant sounds of drilling.
The Latour family has a skeptical but tolerant attitude
toward all this activity; they are cooperative but not hope-
ful of overnight riches. The boy finally realizes what is
happening to his world when the waves from a speeding
boat shake his little canoe so violently that he must jump
into the water to avoid the boat's being capsized.

Next Flaherty establishes one of the most important symbols in a film which is full of symbols. The surveying team
locates a spot for drilling and marks it with a stake in the
water; this stake records their invasion, and soon it is
surrounded by the debris brought down the river by the
drilling barges, then by the derrick itself, and finally by
what is called a Christmas tree, a pumping unit which will
control the flow of oil into the pipelines that will take it to
the refinery. Perhaps the most effective symbol in the film
is the derrick itself, a steel structure of abstract force and
almost spiritual grandeur. The boy first sees it as he is
looking for his raccoon, and the moment in which it enters
his sight is unforgettable. Floating through the flat marshes

173

Above: in contrast to the boy's world of silence and shadows, the man's world is one of powerful oil drilling rigs and bold shapes against the sky.

Left: *Louisiana Story*: this lyrical nonfiction film is told through the eyes of Alexander Napoleon Ulysses Latour, who is happiest when floating in his canoe through the shadowy swamps.

on a yet unseen barge, it towers clean and powerful; the majestic music which accompanies it does not exaggerate the moment. But it is also frightening, for even though it can be seen, its function is not yet clear; and even though it is operated by men, it seems inhuman.

The second sequence of the film is a long, but brilliantly photographed and edited, account of the noisy drilling operations. Here the editing artistry of Helen van Dongen is continually evident. The drilling operation is seen as a thing of great beauty; in fact, the film-making crew referred to this sequence as the ballet of the roughnecks. Each step in the process is explained visually and without narration; frequent cuts to the boy in his boat further emphasize that he regards the drilling rig as a foreign intrusion into his home territory. Here Flaherty's detailed interest in the industrial process is matched by Leacock's inventive photography; the drilling is seen from many angles—from the front, from above, and from the men's eyes. This careful visual explanation is matched by superb sound recording; every noisy step of the drilling process is captured to involve us directly in the activity. We also see the drilling from the boy's viewpoint. He is invited to visit the derrick, and as he becomes friendly with the men he tells them about his magic—his bag of salt and the "something else" (the frog) he keeps hidden in his shirt to frighten "them" when and if such nameless spirits should ever appear.

This introduces the third sequence of the film, where it appears that the huge bayou alligators are "them." The boy and his raccoon are drifting in his canoe, but when the boy beaches the boat and begins to explore the land, he leaves the animal tied in the boat. In a scene of tremendous suspense he finds an alligator's nest and holds a newly hatched

176

alligator in his hand; the enormous mother alligator sees him, crawls slowly from the water, and moves menacingly toward the boy. While the music heightens the suspense and suggests that this exploration will end in tragedy for the boy, the alligator give a warning hiss as it plunges forward, and the boy runs back to safety. Here the photography, editing, and music are perfectly matched. In the bayou the vicious and destructive alligator is one of man's greatest enemies, and at this point Flaherty wins our sympathy by suggesting (through flashbacks) that the alligator has eaten the lovable raccoon, which has disappeared from the boat. In an act of revenge that is more bold than believable, the boy catches an alligator with a large hook (baited with meat and some of his own spit) and then fights the animal in a terrific tug of war; he loses the struggle, but soon after we see him (and his father, who has rushed to his rescue) with the huge alligator skin. This long scene is masterfully edited to capture the excitement of the fight —the boy on one end of a slim rope and the alligator on the other—and it almost succeeds in convincing us that the fight is real. But the frightening scene was staged; as Flaherty once said, "Sometimes you have to lie. One often has to distort a thing to catch its true spirit." But fighting the alligator is the sort of thing this boy would do, and it fits his character whether or not it was staged to protect his safety.

In the fourth sequence the father teases the workers about their failure to strike oil, and their activity comes to a halt with a wildcat blowout of the drilling operation. With a tremendous explosion of gas and salt water all activity at the rig comes to a standstill. When the boy visits this scene, he decides to arouse the "spirit" of the well by dropping some salt down the shaft and spitting after it. The men laugh when he tells them of his belief in magic, and he is both bewildered and hurt. He believes in magic, not in technology, and he wants to prove himself and his ability against the strange and unsuccessful attempts of the men and their machines. The problem is eventually solved by a technique known as slant drilling, and soon the well comes gushing in. Flaherty uses shots of newspaper headlines and stories to inform us of the blowout and the final success. This technique may seem clumsy, but it is quick and it emphasizes the fact that the whole operation is part of a mechanized world, one that is strange and foreign to the calm bayous.

In the concluding sequence the father returns from the city with the usual provisions, but he is also carrying presents for his wife and son, items purchased with the first payment he has received from the oil company. There is a new saucepan and a dress for his wife, and a new rifle for the boy. As the boy goes outside to test the new gun he sees his pet raccoon for the first time since he thought that it had been killed by the alligator. This little reunion helps to round out the structure of the film, for now the boy is together with his friend while the drilling rig leaves as quietly and as impersonally as it arrived. There is peace once more on the water, the boy has a new gun, and the raccoon is back home. One thing is changed, however; the wooden stake has been replaced by the "Christmas tree" pumping unit. The boy sails out to this pipe sprouting from the water, climbs it, and in a final gesture waves good-bye to the departing men. But he also spits into the water, perhaps signifying his belief that it was his magic, not their technology, that brought in the well. He believes in the magical power of his spit, but spitting is also an age-old expression of con-

Louisiana Story: at the end of the film, the boy, reunited with his pet raccoon, sits on the "Christmas tree"
pumping unit and bids farewell to the oil-drilling crew.

tempt, an expression which suggests other interpretations for the ending. Perhaps it is the boy's contempt for the noise and confusion of the drilling; perhaps it is Flaherty's contempt for the machines that he hated all his life. Although Flaherty is obviously not angry at the industrial giant which helped to make his film possible, he closes the film with a smile, a spit, and a wave as the boy says good-bye to the men and to the audience.

The narrative of *Louisiana Story* shows Flaherty at his storytelling best, but the pace, rhythm, structure, and balance of the film are the work of Helen van Dongen, the editor. Flaherty's working habits were well known to her, for she had edited his film *The Land* (1941). She knew that he would shoot footage of anything that appealed to him and then argue constantly with the editor to preserve every last inch of it. In *Louisiana Story* he shot twenty-five times more film than appeared in the final cut of the picture. This is not necessarily wasteful, for most scenes must be shot several times before a director captures one that meets his standards, but it is an unusually high ratio. It could be wasteful when the director does not have a clear idea of what he wants, for if his vision is not clear, his crew cannot be expected to do anything but hope for the best. Since Flaherty did not always know what he wanted, it was his great luck to work with an editor of van Dongen's expertise and experience. She was able to deal with this vast amount of footage, to see the story in it, to cut and reject what was unnecessary, and finally to assemble and shape a film which has a simple, clear structure and a charming appeal. As associate producer she also had the responsibility for supervising the recording of the musical score, and before that she worked with Virgil Thomson, the composer, to insure that the mood she hoped for in editing would be echoed in the music.

Although *Louisiana Story* was an independent production, made on location and far away from the resources of a major studio, it reflects the same kind of close artistic collaboration that characterizes films made in Hollywood. Like John Ford, Robert Flaherty put his faith in reality. Flaherty had his own ideas about what was important, and he must have known that an industrial operation as extensive and as messy as oil drilling is harmful to the environment, but he chose not to tell that story and rather to concentrate on the boy and his reaction to the situation. The story is charming, and so is the style of the film which tells it. Robert Flaherty understood that blend of subject and style, and it is his artistry that makes us see and understand it too.

John Ford and The Grapes of Wrath *(1940)*

From the beginning of his film career in 1914 to its end around 1968 the name John Ford (1895–1973) was synonymous with everything we associate with a great film *auteur*. His long filmography includes some routine Hollywood assignments but also some of the masterpieces of American movie history. His name is often linked with westerns, but he made comedies, adventures, war pictures, adaptations of great novels, and nonfiction films during World War II. He never made a musical, and except for *The Grapes of Wrath* he has not made a major picture about a contemporary social problem. Ford was impatient with those who wanted to talk about his "art" or even the "poetry" of his movies, but, regardless of his humility, he was one of the screen's greatest artists and one of its most eloquent poets. He was also the most honored of American film directors. Ford won four Oscars for directing as well as one Life Tribute Award from the American Film Institute; four times he was named best director by the New York Critics Circle. Equally important in Hollywood, he was a director whose work consistently earned money for the studios which employed him. Ford was always part of the Hollywood movie industry, but he was also independent, accepting his assignments but filming them in his own way. Although Ford fought with producers and writers, he was not an opponent of the studio system, for unlike Flaherty, he achieved his independence within the system. The extraordinary thing about both Flaherty and Ford is their independence, their determination to make films, and their influence on other filmmakers.

When we talk of a filmmaker as a "poet," we mean simply that he has an individual vision of the world and an individual means of expressing it through his films. Flaherty's vision pictured man in conflict with nature, with the physical and natural elements that are both cruel and kind. In each of his five films he shows men learning to live with nature, to cope with its size and splendor. Ford, too, is concerned with man's relationship with physical nature, but his vision is rounded by a further emphasis on man's relations with other men, with what we call human nature. It would be precarious to generalize about his films, but many of the most important ones (and certainly *The Grapes of Wrath*) focus on life as lived in a community (in the largest sense of that word), on the hazards and rewards of human relations, and on human struggle as a necessary element in life. Ford is at his best when he is telling a story that illustrates these characteristics in direct and simple terms.

So while Flaherty and Ford have something in common, they are also separated by many significant factors. As we have seen, they share a common vision, they were both pioneers in movie history, and they are both regarded by those who supported the *auteur* theory as among the most eminent of filmmakers. But the two films under discussion here show their differences. *Louisiana Story* was an independent nonfiction film production, based on Flaherty's own exploration and observation of the bayous. It runs for one hour and twenty minutes, tells a simple story, and is ambiguous in its attitude toward oil drilling. *The Grapes of Wrath* is a major studio production, based on an impressive adaptation of John Steinbeck's great novel. It runs just over two hours, tells a complex story, and leaves few questions unanswered about its attitude toward migrant workers, banks, and the future of farming in this country. Both films are photographed in black and white, both use dialogue and music, both were critically and commercially successful, and both won awards.

But *The Grapes of Wrath* is the greater of the two films. Its story is much more meaningful and relevant to our world; its photography, acting, and effect are far more impressive; and its intentions are considerably more ambitious. Furthermore, the presence and control of John Ford as director are evident in every shot. Ford collaborated with a great studio and with a much larger crew than that which helped Flaherty to make his film, but he rarely lost touch with the production. The entire film, expresses his vision, his care for intimate details, and his intense feeling and love for what he was doing. John Ford was a professional filmmaker throughout his long career; Robert

Flaherty was a storyteller first and a filmmaker second. Each took a different approach to film-making, and each made beautiful films. A closer look at Ford's film will show just how different his approach was.

The Grapes of Wrath was made at Twentieth Century-Fox studios by producer Darryl F. Zanuck; the script was adapted from John Steinbeck's novel by Nunnally Johnson, who also served as associate producer; the director of photography was Gregg Toland; the music was by Alfred Newman. The cast included Henry Fonda (Tom Joad), Jane Darwell (Ma Joad), John Carradine (Casy), Charley Grapewin (Grampa Joad), Dorris Bowdon (Rosasharn) Russell Simpson (Pa Joad), and John Qualen (Muley). The principals of the crew, in addition to those already listed, included an assistant director, two art directors, a set decorator, a film editor, two sound editors, a sound effects director, a sound recorder, and an assistant editor, as well as a large crew. The film was awarded two Oscars from the Academy of Motion Picture Arts and Sciences for Best Film and Best Actress (Jane Darwell); Ford received the New York Film Critics Award as Best Director for 1940; the film was also selected as the Best Picture of the Year by the National Board of Review and the New York Film Critics.

The Grapes of Wrath climaxed an impressive period of creative activity. Between 1935 and the beginning of World War II Ford made *The Informer* (1935), *The Whole Town's Talking* (1935), *Prisoner of Shark Island* (1936), *Mary of Scotland* (1936), *The Plough and the Stars* (1936), *Wee Willie Winkle* (1937), *The Hurricane* (1937), *Four Men and a Prayer* (1938), *Submarine Patrol* (1938), *Stagecoach* (1939), *Young Mr. Lincoln* (1939), *Drums Along the Mo-*

hawk (1939), *The Grapes of Wrath* (1940), *The Long Voyage Home* (1940), *Tobacco Road* (1941), and *How Green Was My Valley* (1941). With two or three exceptions, each of these films is important in one or more ways, and several of them are regarded as masterpieces.

The story of *The Grapes of Wrath* is familiar to almost everyone: the slow disintegration of the Joad family, evicted from their farm land in the dust bowl of Oklahoma, trekking west in search of employment and survival. The story of the family's attempts to stay together and to survive is told against the attempts of larger forces (banks especially but also real estate and agricultural agents and large farmers) to make the most money possible out of a situation that was a national crisis and disgrace. The conflict is basically a simple one: the struggle of a family to keep its unity, its land, and its heritage intact. The Joad family is just one family, but it is also representative of the thousands of uprooted families that suffered and sacrificed during the Great Depression. As Ma Joad says, they "keep a-goin'," and their determination to survive is a metaphor for the struggle of others.

Although Ford's film is a distinguished adaptation of Steinbeck's novel (as well as one of the best films ever made from a novel), it must be considered in itself, as a film, not as a transformation of a work from another medium. As anyone knows who has read the novel and seen the film, there are important differences between the two, and it would be unfair both to Steinbeck and to Ford to discuss them as if they were the same. Ford's version of Steinbeck's novel is simpler in structure, more sentimental, and less controversial in its handling of the ending. Primarily, Ford alters the emphasis of the novel from the Joads' ability

185

to *change* in response to their changing environment to the Joads' ability to *survive* these changes. Considering Steinbeck's emphasis on man's adaptability, that is a striking alteration of the novel. The final point of the movie is different from the conclusion of the novel, and Ford either deletes other characters and scenes or modifies them to fit his conception of the story. Some of the political, religious, and sexual scenes in the novel were cut or tailored to fit the standards set by the Hays Office.

But the greatness of the film comes finally from the rhythm with which Ford controls the development of the story, and from the love and compassion with which he views the Joads. Ford believes in goodness, kindness, and compassion; he believes that people will be decent, productive, and happy if they are merely given the chance; he respects the American virtues of hard work and independence; and he sees the family as the unit which holds all this together. These are his principles in *The Grapes of Wrath*, and each scene develops his conception. The most frequently recurring theme in his films is defeat and failure; he is fascinated with the forces which destroy a man but also with the ways in which that failure can make a hero out of him. The story of the Joad family was a natural one for him to film, and the movie is a texture of small, significant details of human suffering and aspiration. These details are never lost, for they are introduced and illuminated by strong, sensitive performances: Henry Fonda's quiet portrayal of idealistic Tom Joad, Jane Darwell's unforgettable strength as Ma Joad, John Carradine's moving portrayal of the preacher Casy, the haunted character of Muley as brilliantly played by John Qualen. Each reveals a different aspect of suffering and sacrifice and groping toward social justice and equality.

186

Many of these details are of course from the Steinbeck novel, but their choice and arrangement were the responsibility of Darryl F. Zanuck, Nunnally Johnson, and John Ford. The script is not always faithful to the novel, as we have noted, for it leaves much out, but it emphasizes the simple, dignified story and the strong characters.

Although there is actually very little of it, music plays an important part in the film; when it is used, it is perfect. Ford's films rely much less on music than other Hollywood films, and here the music is used not to overwhelm the audience but to underline the softness and sentimentality of the director's vision. The major theme is the American folk ballad "Red River Valley," first played on an accordion as Ma Joad chooses which of her possessions to take along on the journey, then on a guitar at Grampa Joad's funeral, then more brightly on a fiddle as Tom and his mother dance at the government camp, and then again on the accordion as Tom takes his final leave, and finally in a lively orchestral version at the end of the film. The sadness and longing expressed in the song itself are given a note of hope at the end of the film, and the music then helps to point out the difference between the novel and the film. At the end of the novel the Joads are trapped by rising flood waters, Rosasharn has lost her baby and gives the milk from her swollen breasts to a starving tramp, the family's future looks grim. At the end of the movie the Joads are on the road, we don't know about the baby, and the family is heading toward the possibility of twenty days of work. Steinbeck says that the Joads will have to change in order to survive; Ford says that they will survive without changing, and this is emphasized by the theme song that has been theirs throughout the film. Hollywood liked "happy endings," and producer Zanuck wanted to avoid the controversy and censorship that had surrounded the novel, so while Ford's version of the novel is by no means "happy" in the usual sense in which that word is applied to film endings, it does not go contrary to Steinbeck's qualified vision of hope.

The realism of the film is enhanced by three things: the superb acting, the authentic settings, and the beautiful photography. Little is known about the actual production of the film because Zanuck kept it closely guarded for fear of outside controversy. But it appears that most of the film was shot in the studio, and that offers a clue to the beauty of its visual images. The designers purposely sought a stark look in the costumes and in the settings of road camps, farms, and the road itself. The realism of these costumes and settings is captured beautifully by Gregg Toland's photography. Some of the footage is so real-looking that it seems as if newsreel or other nonfiction footage had been incorporated into the film; it was, in fact, all original photography. Toland was one of Hollywood's most accomplished photographers—Ford called him one of the three best cameramen he ever worked with—and here their understanding of one another is evident in almost every shot. Ford sees men like Tom Joad as "men against the sky," lonely men searching for truth in a world that is alien to them. Toland translates this viewpoint into unforgettable photographic images that directly communicate this particular vision. In *The Grapes of Wrath* Toland avoids much of the startlingly innovative photography that was to characterize his work a year later in *Citizen Kane* (1941), no doubt because Ford's requirements—and the nature of the Steinbeck story—were very different from the requirements Orson Welles had in mind for *Citizen Kane*. Here Toland mainly uses medium shots from a straightforward eye-level, but he also shoots some scenes from below (the technique that was to make memorable so much of the photography in *Citizen Kane*.) Generally, he avoids close-ups and long shots, although there are many unforgettable close-ups in the film, and he makes little use of other such familiar techniques as montage and superimposition.

The most striking aspect of Toland's cinematography here is the lighting, and because almost exactly half of the film's action took place at night or under dimly lit conditions, he had a remarkable opportunity for exploiting the possibilities of black-and-white composition. In some scenes there is a strong contrast between these blacks and whites, such as the great scene, shot partly from above, in which Muley squats down and fingers the dust of the farm he has just lost to the banks. In other scenes there is a soft, shadowy quality, such as the scene lit by candles in which Ma Joad goes through her few possessions before leaving her farm for the last time, or the earlier scene lit by one candle in which Muley tells Tom and Casy about the deserted farm. Although this lighting is visually beautiful, its softness tends at times to lessen the impact of the film's blunt, realistic story. But the overall effect of the lighting and the photography is consistent with the sentimentality of Ford's view of this story.

Ford was famous for knowing what he wanted in a shot, and it was seldom necessary for him to reshoot footage. In most projects he used very little film and was so sure of his judgement that there was little for his editors to do but assemble the shots he had made. But in *The Grapes of Wrath* Ford's judgment failed him at times, and his decision to take a vacation and leave the editing to Robert Simpson

189

resulted in several flaws in the film's narrative.

Ford's absence during the editing process was one problem; the producer's interference was another. Because of the opposition to the novel Zanuck was concerned for the success of his film with the public. Not only did he keep his film project safe from controversy during production, but he wanted to get it to the public as quickly as possible. If he had taken more time in supervising the editing, Zanuck would have realized that some shots and scenes needed reshooting, and that some events were not explained in the film. We never know what happens to Rosasharn's baby, or where or why Tom's brother Noah disappears from the film. Of course, these are minor flaws, but they are all the more obvious in a film in which almost everything else is perfect.

The Grapes of Wrath is composed of fifty scenes that are grouped into fifteen sequences. The first sequence is Tom Joad's return; it establishes his isolation and his feelings about the differences between the rich and the poor. Here he meets Casy, the eccentric ex-preacher who has lost his religion, the man who will influence the rest of his life. The second sequence takes place in the deserted Joad farmhouse; it is one of the most beautiful and complex in the film, for it introduces the frightened Muley, who tells the story of the plight of the Oklahoma farm workers. The third sequence shows the Joad family at breakfast, ready to leave for California, and is notable for its sentimental view of family life and for its beautiful portrait of Ma Joad. The fourth sequence details Grampa's death and gives Tom and Casy an opportunity to comment on a poor man's fate in a rich man's country.

Sequence five takes place in a camp ground. Here Rosasharn's husband, Connie, sings "I Ain't A-Gonna Be

The Grapes of Wrath: John Qualen (Muley),
Henry Fonda (Tom Joad), and John Carradine (Casy)
just after Muley has told them how the banks have forced
people off their own land.

The Grapes of Wrath: Russell Simpson (Pa Joad), Frank Darien (Uncle John), Zeffie Tilbury (Granma), Charley Grapewin (Grampa), Jane Darwell (Ma Joad), with other members of the Joad family, at their final breakfast before leaving for California.

A-Treated This A-Way,'' a ballad that foreshadows his even-
tual decision to abandon his pregnant wife and the rest of
the Joad family. Here, also, the men hear the heartbreaking
story of a bitter migrant worker who has been to California,
and whose wife and two children have died there of malnu-
trition. This powerful moment is the first real sign that the
Joads (and the others) are in danger. The sixth sequence
is brief in its picture of the good people at a roadside diner.
The seventh sequence follows the Joads across Arizona,
past Indian villages, toward California. In the eighth sequence they reach the Colorado River, the border between
Arizona and California, but still have to face the long, hot
road through the California desert.

In the ninth sequence the family's plight is made even
more difficult by Granma Joad's illness, and in sequence
ten they reach the greenery of California only to find that
Granma has died. The eleventh sequence brings the Joads
into contact with a policeman who is originally from Oklahoma, but they find that he is not a friend, for he warns them
that migrant workers are not welcome in California.

The next three sequences, set in contrasting California
camps, form the center of the film's thematic focus. In sequence twelve the Joads are in Hooverville, the appalling
camp for migrant workers. For the first time they realize
the magnitude of the migrants' problems as they encounter
starving children, despairing adults, hostile sheriffs, a shooting, and the rumor that vigilantes are preparing to attack
the camp. The thirteenth sequence takes place at the Keene
Ranch, a kind of concentration camp for farm workers who
are willing to work for whatever wages are offered. Outside
the fence a strike is in process; Tom finds Casy involved,
but soon Casy is killed and Tom is accused of killing the

193

man who has murdered his friend. Again the family must hit the road, with Tom concealed in the truck. In the fourteenth sequence the Joads arrive at the Wheat Patch Government Camp, different in every way from Hooverville and the Keene Ranch. Here the film's message becomes apparent: the government must bear the responsibility for protecting the migrants from unprincipled farmers and those who take the law into their own hands. The camp is well-organized, unlike the squalid camps where the family has been forced to stay, and the family enjoys a sense of security, adequate sanitary facilities, Saturday night dances, and some limited work. But this happiness is only temporary, for Tom is being hunted for his part in the scuffle which caused Casy's murder, and he must leave the family. In the fifteenth and final sequence Tom has left and Ma Joad becomes the focus of the film. As the family leaves the government camp in search of work she says the lines that underscore Ford's version of the novel's ending. Her insistence is that the family—and all people like them —will survive. While this notion seems almost contrary to Steinbeck's ending, as well as different from Tom's final speech and Casy's view of things in the film, it does satisfy the producer's need for an acceptable ending.

There are many memorable scenes in the film, all of them a product of the collaboration of director, script writer, actors, photographer, and designers. Among them there is the concise, humorous scene at the beginning in which Tom Joad arrives home; he has just been released from prison, and his family thinks he has "bust out," so he must continually repeat the word "parole" as they gather around him. There is the touching scene in which Ma Joad must decide which of her few possessions to keep and which to

194

leave behind. The things she has saved are sweet reminders of a happier time, and as she goes through them we are deeply touched by the intense emotion of the moment, an emotion which is conveyed without words. Music, Jane Darwell's expressive face, and tight close-ups preserve this scene for memory. And there is the equally powerful scene, touched on briefly above, in which Muley tells Tom and Casy about the "notice" which drove the farmers off their land. Sitting in shadows, he is a man afraid, a man in hiding; this is the opposite of the freedom he and the others have so long enjoyed, as well as a foreshadowing of the ways in which others along the road will make the Joads cringe like animals. Even though they have been poor, they have been free and able to face the world unafraid. Here in flashback we see Muley defeated by the banks and their bulldozers. Squatting down on the dusty land he has just lost, he speaks eloquently of what that land means to him and his family. Part of the scene is shot from above, as already mentioned, so that we see Muley's long, dark shadow across the dry ground.

This theme of the land and its importance is carried throughout the film, but perhaps no more subtly than in the scene in which Grampa Joad dies. He grasps some soil and hands it to his son, almost as if he were passing on the legacy to his own farmland; ironically, he is dying by the side of the road on land that is not his, and the family must bury him in this land as if he were a stranger.

A scene in a roadside cafe is a perfect illustration of another key theme: the value of human kindness. Here Pa Joad asks if he may buy a ten-cent loaf of bread; the bread costs fifteen cents, and the waitress would rather sell sandwiches than bread, but the cook tells her to sell it anyway.

195

But she refuses until a small, impressive thing occurs. Two of the Joad children hungrily eye the candy on display, but it too is beyond their reach. When the waitress understands their longing, she quickly adjusts the price to make it possible for each of them to have a piece. Two truck drivers who are eating in the restaurant tease her about this, but when they leave, they refuse to take the change owed from their bill. Thus people help one another. The cook sells the bread at a price the Joads can afford; the waitress sells the five-cent candy at what she says is two for the price of one cent; and the truck drivers (who, ironically, are driving large moving vans) leave more than enough change to make up the difference, thus demonstrating that a little kindness goes a long way in creating more kindness and happiness. This is a simple, sentimental scene, but it illustrates as effectively as any scene in the film that people's minds are not rigid, that kindness can overcome hardness, and that money is not always an obstacle to happiness.

But John Ford's vision is not all that simple. The film begins with a beautifully photographed image of Tom Joad walking down a lonely country road. Before he reaches home, he will encounter a nosy truck-driver, an eccentric ex-preacher (Casy), and the frightened Muley. It is Muley who reveals and establishes the conflict in the film when he tells Tom and Casy about the "notice" that has evicted them all from their land. In the flashback previously discussed we see the conflict: individual farmers against large banks. But it is in the opening image that Ford has clearly rooted the basic conflict: man against the sky. The wind storm, the isolated house, the physical hardships that the family endures on the trip are all just aspects of this elemental conflict. In the opening scene we see Tom, the desolate farm

196

landscape, a preacher who has lost his faith, a man who has been scared into the shadows of the deserted Joad farmhouse, and we know that the one thing that will keep Tom going, and later keep his family going, is the belief that they can stay together and win their struggle. The outside world is not particularly cruel; after all, bankers have their responsibilities just like everyone else. But their actions seem all the more harsh because they lack any contact with the immediate personal suffering of the individual families whose lives they are changing. On its journey the family continues to meet the clean, well-dressed representatives of society: bankers' agents, gas station attendants, police inspectors. Most of these people are just doing their jobs, but some of them are kind and warm-hearted, like the cook, the waitress, and the truck drivers, as well as the agricultural inspector who allows them to pass even though he sees that Granma Joad is dead. These people are remarkable, but so are the Joads because they never blame anyone for their hardship. Tom reacts strongly to the treatment he and the others are given, and once or twice he threatens violence. And he has one of the strongest speeches in the film when he talks about people who break the spirit of others. That is the one unforgivable cruelty, the one thing that robs a man or woman of dignity and self-respect. The Joads have been hurt, and their frightened eyes say more than they ever do. Here again the photography, lighting, and composition say more than words.

Ford's vision of human kindness and human cruelty is given very strong expression in his (and Steinbeck's) admiration for the efforts made by the United States government to help the migrant workers. In a long scene that is both humorous and touching the Joads arrive at the Wheat

Patch Government Camp run by the Department of Agriculture. The camp is run along democratic lines by the campers themselves, and it provides one of the few periods in the family's journey in which they have a sense of worth and well-being. Here, protected from preying agricultural agents, greedy merchants, and vigilante mobs, they regain their confidence and dignity. Here the Joads are happy, as they must have been in the past, and this is underscored when Tom and Ma dance together to the music of "Red River Valley." But the dance floor which brings them together is also the scene of their final parting. The happiness they share in this camp is not propaganda for the government, for it is made clear that there are very few of these camps and that the migrant workers are subject to continual exploitation. In many ways the story of *The Grapes of Wrath* is as true today as it was in the 1930s, for the problems of migrant farm workers are still largely uncorrected. The situation remains a national disgrace.

But Ford sees the strength of the Joads in their determination to keep going, not in their brief period of happiness in the government camp. At the end of the film Tom Joad leaves the family not because he is afraid of being caught but because he does not want to endanger the other members. He remembers Casy's example—he refers to Casy as a lantern—and vows to his mother that he will go anywhere, do anything, to fight injustice. This scene of parting recalls the moment of reunion between Tom and his mother near the beginning of the film. With the quiet dignity of proud, poor people, Tom and Casy wait in the yard of the house until they are recognized. When Ma Joad runs to greet him, her first remark is to ask if Tom has been "hurt" in prison. To her, and to Tom, this means a hurting of the individual spirit, a breaking of a person's dignity. There is fear in her eyes here, too, as once again she mentions hurt. The hurt and the pain are internal, of course, for their cuts and bruises are minor in contrast to the death of the spirit which they all fear.

After Tom and his mother make their whispered farewells outside their tent at the government camp, he takes his leave by walking across the deserted, quiet outdoor dance floor. We remember the gaiety and fun that took place here just hours before, and as we see Tom leave we are reminded once again of the happy past and the unhappy present. The final image of Tom is even more striking than the opening image: he is walking slowly uphill, silhouetted against the sky, a solitary traveler in search of justice and peace. The family takes to the road again too, but they are not in despair. Their spirits have been restored, and they will keep going, as Ma Joad affirms, because they are the people, the strength of the country. Although they have no land and only a promise of twenty days' work, although their truck is almost a complete wreck, and several members of the family have been lost, the film tells us that their strength, their spirit, and their determination to succeed will insure their survival.

The Grapes of Wrath is John Ford's vision of defeat and sacrifice, of struggle and hope; even though it is based on a famous and familiar novel, it is nonetheless an original vision. The sights, sounds, and shape of his film are the products of his imagination, and they add an unforgettable dimension to the experience of reading the Steinbeck novel.

FOR FURTHER READING

The following titles, grouped according to the three main sections of this book, are only a few of the many available books on film. These have been selected for their interest and appeal to the young reader, and most have been reprinted in paperback editions. For a more complete list of books, see Ronald Gottesman and Harry M. Geduld, *Guidebook to Film*, New York: Holt, Rinehart and Winston, Inc., 1972; Richard Dyer MacCann and Edward S. Perry, *The New Film Index*, New York: E. P. Dutton, 1974; and the appendix in Gerald Mast, *A Short History of the Movies*, 2nd ed., Indianapolis: The Bobbs-Merrill Co., Inc., 1975.

history

BARSAM, RICHARD MERAN. *Nonfiction Film: A Critical History.* New York: E. P. Dutton, 1973.

BROWNLOW, KEVIN. *The Parade's Gone By.* New York: Alfred A. Knopf, Inc., 1968.

DICKINSON, THOROLD and ANTONIA. *A History of the Kinetograph, Kinetoscope, and Kinetophonograph.* New York: Arno Press, 1970.

MAST, GERALD. *A Short History of the Movies.* 2nd ed. Indianapolis: The Bobbs-Merrill Co., Inc., 1975.

RAMSAYE, TERRY. *A Million and One Nights.* New York: Simon & Schuster, 1964.

SARRIS, ANDREW. *The American Cinema: Directors and Directions 1929–1968.* New York: E. P. Dutton, 1968.

YOUNGBLOOD, GENE. *Expanded Cinema.* New York: E. P. Dutton, 1970.

production

CLARKE, CHARLES G. and STRENGE, WALTER, eds. *American Cinematographer Manual.* Hollywood: American Society of Cinematographers, 1973.

CORLISS, RICHARD, ed. *The Hollywood Screenwriters.* New York: Avon Books, 1972.

GESSNER, ROBERT. *The Moving Image: A Guide to Cinematic Literacy.* New York: E. P. Dutton, 1970.

GOLDSTEIN, LAURENCE and KAUFMAN, JAY. *Into Film.* New York: E. P. Dutton, 1976.

HAPPÉ, L. BERNARD. *Basic Motion Picture Technology.* New York: Hastings House Publishers, 1971.

HIGHAM, CHARLES. *Hollywood Cameramen: Sources of Light.* Bloomington, Ind., and London: Indiana University Press, 1970.

MALTIN, LEONARD, ed. *Behind the Camera: The Cinematographer's Art.* New York: New American Library, 1971.

PINCUS, EDWARD. *Guide to Filmmaking.* New York: New American Library, 1969.

REISZ, KAREL and MILLER, GAVIN. *The Technique of Film Editing.* New York: Hastings House Publishers, 1968.

ROBERTS, KENNETH H. and SHARPLES, WIN, JR. *A Primer for Film Making.* New York: Pegasus, 1971.

SPOTTISWODE, RAYMOND, ed. *The Focal Encyclopedia of Film and Television Techniques.* New York: Hastings House Publishers, 1969.

YOUNG, FREDDIE and PETZOLD, PAUL. *The Work of the Motion Picture Cameraman.* New York: Hastings House Publishers, 1972.

CRITICISM

BARSAM, RICHARD MERAN, ed. *Nonfiction Film Theory and Criticism.* New York: Dutton Paperbacks, 1976.

BLUESTONE, GEORGE. *Novels into Film.* Baltimore: Johns Hopkins Press, 1957.

BOGDANOVICH, PETER. *John Ford.* Berkeley and Los Angeles: University of California Press, 1968.

CALDER-MARSHALL, ARTHUR. *The Innocent Eye: The Life of Robert Flaherty.* London: W. H. Allen, 1963.

FRENCH, WARREN. *Filmguide to* The Grapes of Wrath. Bloomington, Ind.: Indiana University Press, 1973.

KAEL, PAULINE. *I Lost It at the Movies.* New York: Bantam, 1966.

———. *Kiss Kiss Bang Bang.* Boston: Little, Brown and Company, 1968.

———. *Reeling.* Boston: Little, Brown and Company, 1976.

MAST, GERALD and COHEN, MARSHALL, eds. *Film Theory and Criticism: Introductory Readings.* New York: Oxford University Press, 1974.

SARRIS, ANDREW. *Confessions of a Cultist: On the Cinema, 1955–1969.* New York: Simon and Schuster, 1970.

———, ed. *Interviews with Film Directors.* New York: Avon Books, 1967.

GENERAL REFERENCE

GEDULD, HARRY M. and GOTTESMAN, RONALD. *An Illustrated Glossary of Film Terms.* New York: Holt, Rinehart and Winston, Inc., 1973.

HALLIWELL, LESLIE. *The Filmgoer's Companion.* New York: Avon Books, 1970.

FOR FURTHER VIEWING

This short selection of the most important films made in the past one hundred years is intended as a mini-catalogue of the film classics that everyone should know. They were selected because of their significance and influence in the development of film technique and style and for their place in film history. The purpose here is to offer a representative outline of film history based on the first section of this book. In this list the title is followed by the name of the director, year of release, and a key to the 16 mm distributor.

A list of the major distributors and their addresses is at the end of this list; their catalogues will give full details, including plots, casts, and rental fees.

silent films

THE BIRTH OF THE MOVIES: FRANCE, USA, BRITAIN

The First Programs and *Early Lumière Films* (Louis and Auguste
  Lumière, 1895–96, MOMA)
Films of the 1890s (Thomas A. Edison, 1894–99, MOMA)
George Méliès Program (George Méliès, 1899–1912, MOMA)
Edwin S. Porter: Five Films (Edwin S. Porter, 1903–07, MOMA)
Ferdinand Zecca Program (Ferdinand Zecca, 1906–07, MOMA)
The Beginnings of the British Film (1901–11, MOMA)

D. W. GRIFFITH

Griffith Biograph Program (1901–11, MOMA)
The Birth of a Nation (1914, MOMA)
Intolerance (1916, MOMA)

WHEN COMEDY WAS KING: SENNETT, CHAPLIN, KEATON

Mack Sennett Program (1911–20, MOMA)
Chaplin's Keystone Films (1914, MOMA)
Chaplin's Essanay Films (1915–16, MOMA)
The Gold Rush (Charles Chaplin, 1925, AUD, EMG, JAN, MED)
Buster Keaton Shorts (1920–23, AUD)
The General (1926, AUD, EMG)

AMERICAN SILENT FEATURES

The Coward (Thomas Ince, 1915, MOMA)
The Last of the Mohicans (Maurice Tourneur, 1920, FCE, MOG)
The Three Musketeers (Douglas Fairbanks, 1921, MOMA)
Foolish Wives (Erich von Stroheim, 1922, EMG, MOMA, UNI)
Blood and Sand (Fred Niblo, 1922, AUD, MED, MOMA)
The Covered Wagon (James Cruze, 1923, AUD, STA)
Greed (Erich von Stroheim, 1924, FI)
The Big Parade (King Vidor, 1925, FI)
Phantom of the Opera (Rupert Julian, 1925, AUD, MED)
Ben Hur (Fred Niblo, 1926, FI)
The Scarlet Letter (Victor Sjøstrøm, 1926, FI)
The Crowd (King Vidor, 1928, FI)

EUROPEAN SILENT FEATURES

The Cabinet of Doctor Caligari (Robert Wiene, Germany, 1920, AUD, EMG, MOMA)
Nosferatu (F. W. Murnau, Germany, 1922, MOMA)
The Joyless Street (G. W. Pabst, Germany, 1925, MOMA)
Metropolis (Fritz Lang, Germany, 1926, JAN, MOMA, STA)
Sunrise (F. W. Murnau, Germany, 1927, EMG, AUD, MOMA)
The Italian Straw Hat (René Clair, France, 1927, CON)
The Passion of Joan of Arc (Carl-Theodore Dreyer, France, 1928, AUD)
Potemkin (Sergei Eisenstein, Russia, 1925, AUD, MOMA)
Mother (Vsevlod I. Pudovkin, Russia, 1926, AUD, MOMA)
The Man With the Movie Camera (Dziga-Vertov, Russia, 1929, AUD)
Earth (Alexander Dovzhenko, Russia, 1930, AUD)

EARLY NONFICTION FILMS

Nanook of the North (Robert Flaherty, USA, 1922, CON, MOMA)
Rien que les heures (Alberto Cavalcanti, France, 1926, MOMA)
Berlin: Symphony of a Great City (Walther Ruttmann, Germany, 1927, MOMA)
Turksib (Victor Turin, Russia, 1929, AUD)

EXPERIMENTAL FILMS

Kino-Pravda (Dziga-Vertov, Russia, 1922, MOMA)
Ballet Mécanique (Fernand Léger, France, 1924, MOMA)
Emak Bakia (Man Ray, France, 1927, AUD, MOMA)
Un Chien Andalou (Luis Buñuel and Salvador Dali, France, 1929, MOMA)

TRANSITION TO SOUND

The Jazz Singer (Alan Crosland, USA, 1927, CON, STA)
Applause (Rouben Mamoulian, USA, 1929, UNI)
The Love Parade (Ernst Lubitsch, USA, 1929, MOMA, UNI)
All Quiet on the Western Front (Lewis Milestone, USA, 1930, SWA, TWY, UNI)
City Lights (Charles Chaplin, USA, 1931, RBC)
M (Fritz Lang, Germany, 1931, AUD, EMG, FCE, JAN)

sound films

EUROPEAN SOUND FILMS: 1930–45

Germany

The Threepenny Opera (G. W. Pabst, 1931, AUD)
France
Le Million (René Clair, 1931, AUD)
The Rules of the Game (Jean Renoir, 1939, JAN)
Zéro de conduite (Jean Vigo, 1933, AUD)
The Children of Paradise (Marcel Carné, 1945, CON)

Russia

Alexander Nevsky (Sergei Eisenstein, 1938, AUD)
Ivan the Terrible (Parts I and II, Sergei Eisenstein, 1946, AUD)

AMERICAN SOUND FILMS: 1930–45

Ninotchka (Ernst Lubitsch, 1939, FI)
The Blue Angel (Josef von Sternberg, 1929, CON, JAN)
Queen Christina (Rouben Mamoulian, 1933, FI)
Casablanca (Michael Curtiz, 1942, AUD, CWF, UA)
Bringing Up Baby (Howard Hawks, 1938, FI)
The Grapes of Wrath (John Ford, 1940, FI, MOMA)
Mr. Smith Goes to Washington (Frank Capra, 1939, AUD, SWA)
Little Caesar (Mervyn LeRoy, 1930, AUD, CON, UA)
Camille (George Cukor, 1936, FI)
Modern Times (Charles Chaplin, 1936, RBC)
Citizen Kane (Orson Welles, 1941, AUD, FI, JAN)
The 39 Steps (Alfred Hitchcock, 1935, FCE, MOG, UFC, WIL)

NONFICTION FILMS: 1930–45

Triumph of the Will (Leni Riefenstahl, Germany, 1935, MOMA)
Night Mail (Harry Watt and Basil Wright, Britain, 1936, MOMA)
The Plow That Broke the Plains (Pare Lorentz, USA, 1937, MOMA)
Olympia (Parts I and II, Leni Riefenstahl, 1938, Germany, CON, MOMA)
The City (Willard van Dyke and Ralph Steiner, 1939, MOMA)
The Land (Robert Flaherty, USA, 1942, MOMA)
Fires Were Started (Humphrey Jennings, Britain, 1943, CON)
Why We Fight (series, Frank Capra, USA, 1943–45, MOMA)

American Films

The Treasure of the Sierra Madre (John Huston, 1948, AUD)
On the Waterfront (Elia Kazan, 1954, AUD, ICS, SWA)
An American in Paris (Vincente Minnelli, 1951, FI)
Anatomy of a Murder (Otto Preminger, 1959, AUD, SWA)
Shane (George Stevens, 1953, FI)
Sunset Boulevard (Billy Wilder, 1950, FI)
The Best Years of Our Lives (William Wyler, 1946, SAM)
High Noon (Fred Zinnemann, 1952, AUD, CON, SWA, TWY)
The Snake Pit (Anatole Litvak, 1948, FI)
All the King's Men (Robert Rossen, 1949, AUD, SWA, TWY)
All About Eve (Joseph L. Mankiewicz, 1950, FI)
The Day the Earth Stood Still (Robert Wise, 1951, FI)
Singin' in the Rain (Stanley Donen and Gene Kelly, 1952, FI)
Marty (Delbert Mann, 1955, UA)
Rebel Without a Cause (Nicholas Ray, 1955, AUD, ICS, SWA, TWF, TWY)
Funny Face (Stanley Donen, 1957, FI)
The Magnificent Seven (John Sturges, 1960, UA)
McCabe and Mrs. Miller (Robert Altman, 1972, WAR)
The Last Picture Show (Peter Bogdanovich, 1971, RBC)
The Godfather (Parts I and II, Francis Ford Coppola, 1972 and 1974, FI)
2001: A Space Odyssey (Stanley Kubrick, 1968, FI)
The Wild Bunch (Sam Peckinpah, 1968, WAR)
The Hustler (Robert Rossen, 1961, FI)
The Manchurian Candidate (John Frankenheimer, 1962, UA)
Whatever Happened to Baby Jane? (Robert Aldrich, 1962, TWY)
Hud (Martin Ritt, 1963, FI)
Who's Afraid of Virginia Woolf? (Mike Nichols, 1966, WAR)
Bonnie and Clyde (Arthur Penn, 1967, ICS, SWA, TWY)
Bullitt (Peter Yates, 1968, ICS, SWA, TWY)
Pretty Poison (Noel Black, 1968, FI)
Easy Rider (Peter Fonda and Dennis Hopper, 1969, RBC)
Medium Cool (Haskell Wexler, 1969, FI)
Butch Cassidy and the Sundance Kid (George Roy Hill, 1969, FI)
Five Easy Pieces (Bob Rafelson, 1970, RBC)

French Films

Diary of a Country Priest (Robert Bresson, 1951, AUD)
The Golden Coach (Jean Renoir, 1953, AUD)
Forbidden Games (René Clément, 1952, JAN)
Diabolique (Henri-Georges Clouzot, 1955, WAR)
Orpheus (Jean Cocteau, 1949, JAN)
Lola Montes (Max Ophuls, 1955, AUD)
Mr. Hulot's Holiday (Jacques Tati, 1953, WAL)
Breathless (Jean-Luc Godard, 1959, CON)
The 400 Blows (François Truffaut, 1959, JAN)
Last Year at Marienbad (Alain Resnais, 1961, AUD)
Les Enfants Terribles (Jean-Pierre Melville, 1950)

Italian Films

Open City (Roberto Rossellini, 1945, CON)
The Bicycle Thief (Vittorio de Sica, 1948, AUD)
La Strada (Federico Fellini, 1954, AUD)
La Terra Trema (Luchino Visconti, 1948, AUD)
L'Avventura, La Notte, L'Eclisse (Michelangelo Antonioni, 1960,
    1961, 1962, JAN, UA, AUD)
Before the Revolution (Bernardo Bertolucci, 1964, AUD)

Swedish Films

The Magician (Ingmar Bergman, 1959, JAN)

British Films

This Sporting Life (Lindsay Anderson, 1963, TWY)
Room at the Top (Jack Clayton, 1959, WAL)
A Hard Day's Night (Richard Lester, 1964, UA)
Henry V (Laurence Olivier, 1944, AUD, TWY)
The Third Man (Carol Reed, 1950, TWY, WAL)
Tom Jones (Tony Richardson, 1963)
Sons and Lovers (Jack Cardiff, 1960, FI)
The Lavender Hill Mob (Charles Crichton, 1951, CON, TWF,
    TWY)
Saturday Night and Sunday Morning (Karel Reisz, 1961, WAL)

Japanese Films

Rashomon (Akira Kurosawa, 1950, JAN)
Ugetsu (Kenji Mizoguchi, 1953, JAN)

Indian Films

Pather Panchali, Aparajito, The World of Apu (Satyajit Ray, 1955, 1956, 1958, AUD)

Miscellaneous European Films

Loves of a Blonde (Miloš Forman, 1965, AUD)
The Shop on Main Street (Jan Kadár and Elmar Klos, 1965, AUD)
Knife in the Water (Roman Polanski, 1962, JAN)
Intimate Lighting (Ivan Passer, 1965, AUD)
The Discreet Charm of the Bourgeoisie (Luis Buñuel, 1972, FI)

NONFICTION FILMS

The Sorrow and the Pity (Marcel Ophuls, France, 1971, CIN)
High School (Frederick Wiseman, USA, 1969, ZIP)
Salesman (Alfred and David Maysles and Charlotte Zwerin, USA, 1969, CIN)

EXPERIMENTAL FILMS

Dog Star Man (Stan Brakhage, USA, 1964, FMC)
Scorpio Rising (Kenneth Anger, USA, 1964, FMC)
The Chelsea Girls (Andy Warhol, USA, 1966, AND)
Relativity (Ed Emshwiller, USA, 1966, FMC)
Lemon (Hollis Frampton, USA, 1969, MOMA)
Hallelujah the Hills (Adolfas Mekas, USA, 1963, JAN)

16 MM distributors

AND Warhol Films, Inc.
33 Union Square West
New York, NY 10003

AUD Audio-Brandon Films
34 MacQuesten Parkway
South
Mount Vernon, NY
10550

AUD *or*
1619 North Cherokee
Los Angeles, CA 90028
or
3868 Piedmont Avenue
Oakland, CA 94611
or
8400 Brookfield Avenue
Brookfield, IL 60513

CFS Creative Film Society
8435 Geyser Avenue
Northridge, CA 93124

CIN Cinema 5 & Cinema 16
595 Madison Avenue
New York, NY 10022

CON Contemporary Films/
McGraw-Hill
Princeton Road
Hightstown, NJ 08520
or
828 Custer Avenue
Evanston, IL 60202
or
1714 Stockton Street
San Francisco, CA
94133

CWF Clem Williams Films
2240 Nobleston Road
Pittsburgh, PA 15205
or
5424 West North Avenue
Chicago, IL 60639

DIS Walt Disney Productions
800 Sonora Avenue
Glendale, CA 91201

EMG Em Gee Film Library
16024 Ventura Boule-
vard
Encino, CA 94136

FCE Film Classic Exchange
1926 S. Vermont Avenue
Los Angeles, CA 90007

FI Films Incorporated
35–01 Queens Boulevard
Long Island City, NY
11101
or
4420 Oakton Street
Skokie, IL 60076
or
Offices in Atlanta, Bos-
ton, Dallas, Holly-
wood, Salt Lake City,
and San Diego

FMC Filmmakers' Cooperative
175 Lexington Avenue
New York, NY 10016

GRO Grove Press Films
53 East 11th Street
New York, NY 10003

HUR Hurlock Cine World
13 Arcadia Road
Old Greenwich, CT
06870

ICS Institutional Cinema
Service
915 Broadway
New York, NY 10010

JAN Janus Films
745 Fifth Avenue
New York, NY 10022

MED Media International
107 North Franklin
Street
Madison, WI 53703

MOD Modern Sound Pictures
1410 Howard Street
Omaha, NB 68102

MOG Mogull's
112 West 48th Street
New York, NY 10019

MOMA Museum of Modern Art
Department of Film
11 West 53rd Street
New York, NY 10019

NYF New Yorker Films
43 West 61st Street
New York, NY 10023

RBC RBC Films
933 North LaBrea Ave-
nue
Los Angeles, CA 90038

SAM Samuel Goldwyn 16
1041 North Formosa
Avenue
Los Angeles, CA 90046

STA   Standard Film Service
14710 West Warren
   Avenue
Dearborn, MI 48126

SWA   Swank Motion Pictures
201 South Jefferson
   Avenue
St. Louis, MS 63166

TWF   Trans-World Films
332 South Michigan
   Avenue
Chicago, IL 60604

TWY   Twyman Films
329 Salem Avenue
Dayton, OH 45401

UA   United Artists Sixteen
729 Seventh Avenue
New York, NY 10019

UFC   United Films
1425 South Main Street
Tulsa, OK 74119

UNI   Universal Sixteen
221 Park Avenue South
New York, NY 10003

UNI   *or*
1025 North Highland
   Avenue
Los Angeles, CA 90038
or
425 North Michigan
   Avenue
Chicago, IL 60611
or
Offices in Atlanta, Dallas, and Portland,
Oregon

WAL   Walter Reade 16
241 East 34th Street
New York, NY 10016

WAR   Warner Brothers Film
   Gallery
4000 Warner Boulevard
Burbank, CA 91522

WIL   Willoughby-Peerless
110 West 32nd Street
New York, NY 10001

ZIP   Zipporah Films
54 Lewis Wharf
Boston, MA 02110

index

(Page numbers in italics refer to illustrations.)